"No strings." His eyes moved over her face. "No commitment."

He didn't have to keep spelling it out as if she were some dewy-eyed teenager. She hadn't thought for one moment that he felt anything more for her than a transitory physical desire.

"You haven't slept with anyone since Simon, have you?"

"That is none of your damn business!" Regardless of her response, he was the one who had instigated the kiss, not her. And he was the one who had drawn back first, a taunting little voice reminded her.

"No, it isn't," he agreed. "Would you like your strawberries now?" He glanced over a broad shoulder. "I've some ice cream in the freezer."

"Give mine to the twins," she said curtly.

"What do you want me to do?" he said quietly, his eyes moving over her rigid face. "Apologize for kissing you?"

"Don't be so ridiculous."

"Or apologize for not taking you to bed?"

"I don't want a casual, meaningless affair with you, and I certainly don't want anything more, if that's what you're so terrified of," she said steadily, her eyes never wavering from his. "But I had hoped we might be friends. I was wrong," she concluded simply, and started to walk toward the door.

Rosemary Gibson was born in Egypt. She spent the early part of her childhood in Greece and Vietnam, and now lives in the New Forest. She has had numerous jobs, ranging from working with handicapped children and collecting litter, to being a gas-station attendant and airline ground hostess, but she has always wanted to be a writer. She was lucky enough to have her first short story accepted eight years ago and now writes full-time. She enjoys swimming, playing hockey, gardening and traveling.

Books by Rosemary Gibson

Don't miss any of our special offers. Write to us at the following address for information on our newest releases.

Harlequin Reader Service
U.S.: 3010 Walden Ave., P.O. Box 1325, Buffalo, NY 14269
Canadian: P.O. Box 609, Fort Erie, Ont. L2A 5X3

Last Chance Marriage
Rosemary Gibson

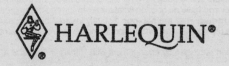

TORONTO • NEW YORK • LONDON
AMSTERDAM • PARIS • SYDNEY • HAMBURG
STOCKHOLM • ATHENS • TOKYO • MILAN • MADRID
PRAGUE • WARSAW • BUDAPEST • AUCKLAND

ISBN 0-373-03514-4

LAST CHANCE MARRIAGE

First North American Publication 1998.

Copyright © 1998 by Rosemary Gibson.

CHAPTER ONE

WEED or seedling? Trowel in her hand, Clemency crouched over the green shoots with thoughtful grey eyes. She'd scattered a packet of mixed annuals around about here in a fit of horticultural zeal last October, she recalled. Leave them alone and see what happens, she decided tranquilly, the spring sunshine glinting on her short copper curls multiplying the smattering of tiny freckles across her neat, straight nose. It was hotter than she'd realised. Dropping the trowel, she picked up the wide-brimmed sun hat that she'd discarded earlier and placed it firmly back on her head.

'Dammit all, I moved down here to the country for some peace and quiet!'

Startled, Clemency rocked back on her heels and then realised that the deep, vehement male voice wasn't addressing her, but issuing from the other side of the thick, high boundary hedge.

'Peace!' There was a loud, derisive snort. 'I've been here barely one week and already every prying, interfering female in the village—no, the whole of Dorset—has been round...'

'Now, stop exaggerating, Joshua, dear,' a serene female voice broke in, adding musingly, 'And I rather thought you moved here to be nearer to your father and I.'

'Handing out advice, offering to babysit for the twins,

5

suggesting I join this, that and the other club...' There was the rhythmic sound of sawing.

'They're just being kind, dear. Welcoming you into the community.'

'I have no desire to be part of the community, absolutely no desire to take up bell ringing, join the wine tasting circle, the gardening club or the local amateur dramatics association...'

Clemency raised her eyebrows, pushing the large sunglasses back on the bridge of her nose. The local societies would probably survive without him, she thought. Feeling a little uncomfortable eavesdropping, even though it wasn't intentional, she tugged up a dandelion and rose to her feet, brushing off the mud from the knees of her jeans.

'What's your neighbour like?' said the female voice.

Another disdainful snort. 'Single. Chartered accountant. Works for a commercial bank in Poole.'

Clemency's mouth curved as she tossed the dandelion into the bucket. The good old village grapevine.

'No male in evidence. Compensates for her lack of social life by working long hours. Mid-twenties with her biological body clock beginning to start ticking.'

Well, really! Indignation and amusement warred for supremacy as Clemency picked up her trowel and bucket of weeds.

'You've met her? That top branch looks dead too, dear.'

'Not as such. She appeared on the doorstep yesterday morning with Jamie's football. Why the hell she couldn't have just tossed it back over the hedge...'

Clemency's eyes sparked. Because she'd decided that it was about time she made some sort of welcoming gesture to her new neighbours, and also let them know that they were perfectly free to come and collect stray balls at any time.

'I didn't bother to answer the door and she left the ball on the front step.'

There was a little sigh. 'You were always so polite as a boy, Joshua.'

'And I saw her peeping at us from an upstairs window yesterday evening.'

She'd been closing her window, that was all, had done nothing more than glance into the next-door garden at the tall, dark-haired man playing cricket with two identical small boys. Pity that he'd chosen that precise minute to glance up. Clemency looked thoughtfully down at her trowel and decided regretfully that it might well miss the intended target.

'Don't you think you're being a little arrogant, dear? Assuming every single woman has designs on you?'

Clemency's eyes danced with repressed, delighted laughter.

'It's not me they have designs on. It's the twins. I'm just part of the package.' There was a fleeting note of self-mockery in the deep voice and then it hardened again. 'The twins are not looking for a mother and I most certainly am not looking for a wife. This is an all-male household and that's the way it intends staying.'

Clemency gave a muffled snort. What sane woman would want to infiltrate that household?

'Yes, dear. When your father gets back from swimming with the twins, I should ask him to have a look at that wisdom tooth.'

'Dad won't want to go into his surgery on a Sunday

afternoon. I'll make an appointment with him for to-morrow.'

'He was planning to go in anyway for a couple of hours to catch up on some paperwork, and you might be able to last out until tomorrow but I don't know whether the rest of us can.'

There was a moment's silence and then the stillness was broken by a rich, deep chuckle. 'Have I been that impossible this morning?'

'You haven't exactly been suffering in silence,' the gentle voice observed dryly, but the underlying affection was marked. 'Shall I hold the ladder?'

Forewarned, Clemency had plenty of time to beat a hasty retreat, but refused to be driven out of her own garden and glanced up with a sunny smile as a dark head and wide, powerful shoulders appeared in her line of vision through the branches of the huge ash tree.

'Hello,' she began cheerfully, and stopped, her breath catching in her throat, the hairs stiffening on the back of her neck as she absorbed the hard, chiselled male features.

It couldn't be him.

Slowly she expelled her breath, berating herself for her idiocy. Even after all these years, she thought wryly, the sudden glimpse of a well-shaped head, of a square, tenacious chin, a certain inflection in a deep male voice could still catch her completely off-guard, could still make some part of her leap in half-remembered recognition.

But of course this man wasn't *him*. That other man belonged to the past, and she'd known that night they'd parted that she would never see him again.

Her eyes jerked upwards again. There was a slight

facial resemblance, that was all, she convinced herself uneasily, but this man looked tougher, more formidable. His face could have been carved out of granite, gave nothing away, the hard, unyielding contours etched by a world-weary cynicism.

'Clemency Adams,' she introduced herself swiftly. Mid-thirties, she judged. It couldn't be *him*, she denied again. It was impossible. He *could not* be her new neighbour. She wasn't even sure how clear her recollection of him was any more, anyway. The image of the dark face still haunted her sleep sometimes but, when she woke with that inexplicable aching sense of loss, the image had blurred. Their time together had been so fleeting.

If he'd noticed her momentary agitation, he gave no indication of it, the blue eyes showing no more than idle curiosity as they swept speculatively down the length of her slight frame from the top of her sun hat, over the baggy pink T-shirt, to her sandalled feet with a dismissive assurance that made her stiffen with inexplicable resentment. He wasn't sure whether she'd heard or not. Didn't much care if she had.

'Joshua Harrington,' he returned crisply, the straight mouth unsmiling. The bare arms revealed by the short-sleeved blue shirt were as tanned as the strong, lean fingers holding the saw.

'How are you settling in?' she enquired blithely, her heart giving an uncomfortable thud. So *that* was his name. 'I'm sure you'll enjoy village life, being part of such a small, friendly, close-knit community.'

The corners of the firm mouth quirked, the unexpected smile transforming the harsh, forbidding face so dramatically that Clemency's stomach turned an involuntary somersault, the terrible, unwelcome sense of familiarity gripping her again, this time leaving her in no doubt—it was him.

'I'm sure I shall, Miss Adams,' Joshua Harrington drawled, the amusement in the discerning blue eyes leaving her in no doubt that he knew she'd overheard his earlier tirade and was now deliberately baiting him.

'Mrs Adams,' Clemency corrected immediately, wondering why on earth she had done so. When she'd first moved to the village, to her intense relief, it had been generally assumed that she was unmarried. She'd neither confirmed nor denied the mistaken assumption, just grateful to be spared the necessity of explaining about Simon.

'Mrs Adams,' he repeated slowly, the blue gaze concentrated on her face with heart-stopping intensity, as if, for the first time, he was mentally stripping her of the camouflaging hat and sunglasses. His mouth suddenly tightened, his eyes narrowing as they lingered on the short copper curls peeping out from beneath the wide-brimmed hat, and then abruptly he turned away, the muscles in his shoulders tautening as he swiftly and efficiently began sawing through the rotten wood.

Averting her own gaze just as abruptly, Clemency pushed the wheelbarrow to the end of the garden to empty the contents. She'd corrected Joshua Harrington because being dismissed as a workaholic spinster had struck a raw nerve, she admitted slowly. Especially as there was more than a grain of truth in it.

Work, initially an antidote to Simon, had slowly come to dominate her entire life to the exclusion of all else, she reflected with uncomfortable honesty. She squared her small chin. Well, unlike her marriage, she was at least making a success of her career, had heard only on

Friday that she'd been short-listed for the vacancy in the international audit team, invited for a second interview in London next week.

The chief attraction of the coveted post was the travel involved. Mostly in Europe, but with occasional trips to Canada, Australia and the Far East. A chance to see much of the world, all expenses paid. Determinedly Clemency tried to recapture the enthusiasm that had made her apply for the position in the first place but was aware only of a tiny, dull emptiness inside her. No one to miss her when she went overseas, no one to greet her rapturously when she returned from each trip.

Snap out of it, Clemency! She could block off Joshua Harrington's words but it was impossible to dismiss the man himself.

Stretched out lazily on the lounger after a late lunch, she tried to concentrate on her novel, but the disturbing image of strong, assured male features seemed to be superimposed on every page. It was all too easy to understand how his advent in the village had made such an impact on the local female populace, she conceded uneasily, overwhelmingly grateful that she was now safely immune to all members of the male sex. Her stomach started to churn; her hands felt clammy. Had he recognised her? She squeezed her eyes shut. Was he divorced? Widowed?

'Hello.'

Her eyes shot open. Two small boys, distinguishable only by the differing colours of their T-shirts, stood by the lounger, studying her solemnly.

'Hello,' she returned with equal gravity, pushing herself upright. About four years old, she hazarded. No, she thought, her stomach muscles constricting. She didn't need to guess—knew almost to the week exactly how old Joshua Harrington's sons were.

'What are you doing?' Red T-shirt enquired, removing a twig from his tousled dark hair.

Thinking about your daddy. 'Reading,' Clemency said firmly.

'Why?'

She was momentarily nonplussed. 'Because I like reading.'

'I can read. What's your name?'

'Clemency. What's your name?'

'Jamie.'

'I'm Tommy.' Blue T-shirt chipped in, looking down admiringly at the grass stains on his jeans.

'Does your daddy know where you are?' Clemency asked gently. Silly question. She hardly imagined Joshua Harrington had passively watched his offspring tunnelling their way through the hedge into her garden.

'He's gone out with Grandpa.'

Of course. The wisdom tooth.

'And Granny's making a cake.'

Doubtlessly innocent of the fact that her two enchanting grandsons had decided to go exploring. Swinging her long, slim legs to the floor, Clemency slipped on her sandals and rose to her feet. The sooner she herded these two escapees home, the better.

'Why?' both Tommy and Jamie enquired in unison when she explained her intention.

'Because your Granny will worry when she finds you're missing.'

'She won't mind,' Tommy said airily. 'Have you got a cat?'

Clemency's lips twitched. Somehow she didn't quite share his optimism. 'No.'

'Anna has two cats,' he informed her, adding grandly, 'When I'm big, I'm going to have ten cats.'

Who was Anna? 'Are you?' Clemency murmured, looking suitably impressed as she guided the two small boys down her front path and up the drive of the adjacent cottage. Originally a farm labourer's dwelling, like her own, it had been extended by a previous owner but still retained its simple charm.

'Have you got a dog?' Jamie took over the interrogation.

'No.'

'Why not?'

'Because it wouldn't be fair to leave it on its own all day while I go to work.'

'My daddy doesn't go to work.'

'He just draws,' Tommy contributed vaguely.

'Does he?' Clemency said casually, determinedly masking her curiosity as she pressed the doorbell.

The woman who answered the door matched the voice she'd heard earlier to perfection. Slight, her dark hair sprinkled with grey, her gentle, serene face evinced momentary surprise and concern.

'What have you two scamps been up to?'

'We've been next door to see Clemency,' Tommy announced innocently.

His grandmother frowned. 'That was very naughty of you both,' she said quietly. 'You know very well you're never to leave the garden on your own.'

'Forgot.' Tommy shuffled his feet uncomfortably and scurried into the cottage.

'Sorry,' mumbled Jamie, his small face equally crest-fallen, and hurried after his twin.

Pulling a rueful face, the older woman held out a hand. 'Mary Harrington. Thanks for bringing them home.'

'Clemency Adams.' Clemency shook the outstretched hand. 'I think there must be a hole in the hedge somewhere.'

'My son's in the process of refencing the garden so it shouldn't happen again. I hope they didn't trample all over the flower beds.'

'With the state of my garden at the moment, I wouldn't notice if a herd of elephants had passed through.' Clemency grinned. 'It's just that there's an old well right at the bottom. There's a small protective wall around it and a manhole cover, but...'

'It might prove irresistible for two curious, unsupervised four-year-olds?' Mary Harrington smiled back. 'Look, I've just made a pot of tea. Have you time to join me in a cup?'

Not wanting to refuse the friendly invitation but reluctant to be discovered ensconced in his home should Joshua Harrington appear, Clemency hesitated and then accepted, following her hostess down the hall into the kitchen overlooking the rambling back garden. Tommy and Jamie, crouched down on their small haunches, were engrossed in a game involving three plastic flowerpots, two sticks and a length of old hosepipe, the rules of which were completely incomprehensible to their two observers.

'Do sit down,' Mary Harrington waved a hand in the general direction of the large refectory table, and poured out two cups of tea. 'Just push some of that clutter to one side,' she added cheerfully.

Removing a plastic spade and bucket from a stool, Clemency drew it up to the table, carefully depositing a toy fire engine and packet of crayons on top of a pile of papers. Twice the size of her own immaculate kitchen, the comfortable, untidy, sun-filled room was evidently a focal point of family life. Brightly crayoned drawings adorned one wall.

'Thank you.' Clemency took hold of the proffered cup and saucer, her mouth curving as her eyes alighted on one of the drawings. Unlike the others, this had evidently been executed by an adult hand. A small boy, easily recognisable as one of the twins, was surrounded by cartoon cats, their almost-human feline expressions indicating their individual characteristics. Lazy, curious, supercilious, artful.

'Joshua drew it for Tommy.' The older woman smiled as she followed Clemency's gaze. Positioning her chair so that she could keep a vigilant eye on her grandsons, she sat down.

'It's very good.' Clemency's eyebrows furrowed together as she continued to study the cartoon. More than good. Professional. There was something familiar in the style. 'My daddy doesn't go to work'. 'He just draws'. A small suspicion beginning to unfurl in her head, her eyes dropped to the pile of papers on her right, editions of the same national daily she had delivered to her cottage. And each morning the first thing she glanced at was the gently satirical topical cartoon on the front page. Josh. She'd always assumed it was a pseudonym—'josh,' as in to tease good-naturedly. But it could equally be the diminutive for Joshua. No. It was all just coincidence. She was adding two and two and making five.

Aware of Mary Harrington watching her, she glanced up and read the confirmation of her unspoken question on the gentle face.

'I always buy *The Best of Josh* every Christmas.' Clemency instantly regretted the unthinking admission, hoping it wouldn't be relayed to the author of the books that usually dominated the bestseller lists each festive season.

'I inundate friends and relatives with copies. And always leave one in the waiting room of my husband's dental practice,' Mary Harrington confessed conspiratorially, and smiled. 'Unbeknown to my son.'

Clemency laughed, liking the warm, unpretentious woman more and more by the second, her laughter suddenly dying in her throat as she heard the key in the door. Simultaneously the twins, having evidently heard a car draw up in the drive, hurtled into the kitchen.

'Daddy's back...'

As the lean figure loomed in the doorway, they launched themselves joyfully towards him like small, exuberant puppies.

'Had a good afternoon?'

The gentleness in Joshua Harrington's voice made Clemency's heart miss an unsteady beat, her eyes leaping to his face. Mesmerised she watched the uncompromisingly male features warm, soften as he rumpled the two small, dark heads, the cynicism temporarily eradicated from his face.

'Yes, Daddy,' the twins chorused enthusiastically, and scampered back out into the garden.

'Mrs Adams.'

Caught completely off-balance, Clemency flushed slightly as Joshua Harrington acknowledged her presence in his home and turned towards his mother. 'Dad'll be back in about an hour,' he relayed, but the dark, slanted eyebrow clearly enquired, What's she doing here?

Or perhaps she was merely being super-sensitive, Clemency acknowledged. She was twenty-seven, had been brought up with three elder brothers, been married, her colleagues were predominantly male—and yet this man unnerved her completely. Even during her adolescence she'd never felt this self-conscious in a man's presence.

'The twins went AWOL and Clemency brought them home,' Mary Harrington said peacefully. 'Tea in the pot. Oh, Lord, the cake!' Springing to her feet, she moved across the kitchen to the stove at the far end.

'Thank you.' The blue gaze flicked to Clemency.

'I considered simply tossing them back over the hedge,' she couldn't resist murmuring with an impish grin, recalling his earlier remark about the football, and instantly regretted it as she saw him frown. She was only joking, for heaven's sake. Being deliberately flip to conceal her fast-fading composure. Then with an uncomfortable jolt she realised that the flippant remark hadn't even registered with him; his whole concentration was focused on her face. He was inspecting each delicate feature, her high, fragile cheekbones, wide-spaced eyes, straight freckle-dusted nose with a clinical thoroughness that she was too keyed up to resent.

There was no acknowledgement of her fragile feminine attraction in the shadowed blue depths, no trace of the appreciation she was accustomed to witnessing—and rebuffing—in male eyes, but something else... But before she could analyse it, before she could be a hundred per cent sure, he had turned away.

Swallowing hard to ease the dryness in her throat, she watched him pour out a mug of tea and carry it across to the table. Removing a cricket bat from a chair, he sat down, stretching his long, lean legs out in front of him.

'How long have you lived in the village, Mrs Adams?' he enquired quietly.

Clemency hesitated. It was a perfectly innocuous question and yet there was something in the astute blue eyes that reflected more than just polite, idle curiosity.

'I moved down here over four years ago.'

'From London?'

Her spine stiffened. 'Yes,' she acknowledged.

'An unusual career move,' he observed slowly.

For a second Clemency wondered if he was baiting her, but there was no hint of mockery in the pensive eyes.

'Relocation,' she said shortly. Relocation of her life.

She focused her attention firmly on Mary Harrington as she rejoined them at the table but it was impossible to distance herself from the formidable male presence on her left. Contributing little to the casual conversation, he nevertheless seemed to dominate the room, emanated a masculine force that was almost tangible.

He wasn't even in her direct line of vision, but she was alert to his slightest movement, her senses tuned into him as if she'd suddenly developed a set of ultra-sensitive antennae.

The kitchen which had seemed so warm and welcoming when she'd first entered seemed to have undergone some subtle change. There was an underlying tension which wasn't solely contributable to her own growing unease. Unable to resist any longer, she flicked the silent man a sideways glance.

Dark eyebrows drawn together, he was frowning at the opposite wall. Unobserved, her eyes swept over the strong planes of his face, and dropped to the firm line of his chiselled mouth.

Unsteadily she picked up her cup and drained the contents, setting it down on the saucer with a clatter that seemed deafening in the otherwise silent kitchen.

'Thanks for the tea.' She forced herself to smile across the table.

'You're more than welcome.' Mary Harrington smiled back.

'I'll see you out.' Her son rose to his feet in a swift, controlled movement.

'Thank you,' she murmured evenly, overwhelmingly conscious of his height and breadth as he ushered her down the hall. Opening the front door, he stood back to enable her to step through, and for an imperceptible second her eyes locked with his, saw the hard certainty in their depths as they raked her oval face. The pretence was over for both of them.

'It was you, wasn't it?' Joshua Harrington said quietly.

The colour drained from her cheeks. 'Yes,' she said simply, and saw a muscle clench along the hard line of his jaw.

'I think I recognised you almost straight away,' he conceded slowly.

'But you hoped you'd made a mistake?' she said levelly.

'Yes,' he admitted shortly.

That swift pinprick of hurt was completely irrational. Hadn't she been equally reluctant to acknowledge his identity? Exhibited no more warmth or pleasure at seeing him again than he had her?

'Your hair was longer then,' he said abruptly.

Five years ago her waist-length red hair had been the most striking, most immediately noticeable thing about her.

'I had it cut.' She stated the obvious, wondering why it should matter that he made no immediate comment on the shorter gamine style. His own physical appearance had altered, too, but the change was more subtle. His dark hair was as thick and rich as she remembered. His eyes were the same intense blue—but the guarded detachment in their depths was as alien to her as the cynicism.

Clemency surveyed him with large, wary eyes, the constrained silence that had fallen between them unbearable. It seemed impossible that she had once, for a short time, felt closer to this man than any other living creature. But she was at a total loss how to even try to bridge the chasm that existed between them now. Wasn't even sure that she wanted to.

'I'd better be getting home.' With amazement Clemency registered her calm, collected voice. But then over the past five years she'd become an expert at concealing her emotions. *What happened to your wife?* Knowing just how tenuous her composure was, terrified that the façade might crack at any minute and she would give utterance to the question pounding in her head, Clemency turned away quickly.

'Mind the step.'

Instinctively he stretched out a hand to steady her as

she missed her footing. His touch was brief and impersonal but her bare skin felt as if it had been scorched.
That she could still react to his slightest touch like this
was ultimately the biggest shock of all.

'Goodbye, Clemency,' he said quietly. It was the first
time he had ever used her given name.

'Goodbye,' she returned, registering the finality in his
voice that told her as clearly as words that he had neither
the desire nor the intention of furthering their acquaintance.

But then, what had she expected? Clemency wondered, her legs swinging with uncharacteristic jerkiness
down the drive. An invitation to come over for coffee
that evening when the twins were in bed to have a cosy
chat about old times?

To Joshua Harrington she would always be a reminder
of a past that, like her, he wanted to forget. A reminder
to that strong, proud, private man of a rare moment of
weakness. Moving on autopilot, Clemency made her
way around to the back of her cottage. Reaching the far
end of her garden without any real recollection of how
she'd arrived there, she sat down on the grass beneath
the shade of an old gnarled apple tree.

Joshua Harrington. A man she had never expected to
see again. The only person to whom she'd ever told the
truth about Simon. Her anonymous confidant. The
stranger on a train.

Except that she hadn't met Joshua Harrington on a
train but on a London bench by the Thames on a dark
New Year's Eve, five years ago.

CHAPTER TWO

DRAWING up her long legs to her chest, Clemency rested her chin on her knees and stared unseeingly at the daisy-strewn lawn. Married to Simon for eighteen months, she'd been so happy at the start of the evening, so totally unprepared for the bombshell that was to wreck her secure world. Her eyes closed. They had been celebrating the end of the year at a party in her eldest brother's flat by the river in Chelsea.

Her hair swinging over her shoulders, cheeks flushed from the heat generating from the swirling, gyrating dancers packed into the small room, Clemency tried unsuccessfully to match the flamboyant steps of her extrovert partner.

As the music slowed, somewhat to her relief, the russet-headed young man took hold of her hand and swung her in front of him.

'I think you're the most beautiful woman here tonight, Clemency Adams,' he proclaimed loudly.

Clemency laughed up into his open, good-natured face.

'And I think you're extremely drunk,' she reproved him affectionately. Best man at their wedding and, like Simon, a school friend of her youngest brother, she'd known David Mason almost all her life.

'Run away with me to my South Sea island home,' he implored her theatrically.

22

'To your bedsit in Clapham?' she teased gently.

'Oh, Clem, you're a hard woman.'

'I'm also a very married one.' She grinned back, her eyes moving around the densely packed room, searching for one particular fair head. There he was. Standing over by the corner talking animatedly to Lisa.

That was an encouraging sign, she thought with satisfaction. Why her husband and her closest friend, two of the people she cared most about in the world, should have developed such an aversion to each other's company over the past few months, after years of friendship, had both baffled and upset her. Hopefully tonight they'd finally decided to call a truce, stop the ridiculous bickering. She felt a wash of sadness as her gaze rested on the small brunette by her husband's side. She was going to miss Lisa when she moved to New York, was still surprised at her sudden decision to apply for the overseas post.

She lost sight of her husband and friend as the tempo of the music increased, dancing with renewed energy until she finally pleaded for mercy from her inexhaustible partner.

'No staying power, these married women,' David teased her, planting a brotherly kiss on her cheek as he released her hand. 'And, if you're looking for your lucky swine of a husband, I just saw him heading towards the kitchen.'

No doubt to replenish his empty glass. Edging her way towards the door, Clemency watched with amusement as David threaded purposefully across the room towards a solitary, attractive blonde. She'd spent the early part of the night circulating, catching up with friends, and now, she thought contentedly as she made her way towards the kitchen, she just wanted to spend what was left of the old year with Simon.

Later she was never quite sure why she had paused in the doorway, had not simply walked straight in the moment she'd seen Simon and Lisa in the otherwise empty kitchen. But she had paused, had seen that expression of utter desolation on Simon's face as he gazed longingly across the room at the dark-haired girl standing with her back to him staring out of the window into the darkness.

'Please don't go to New York, Lissy.'

Clemency froze, unable to move, the anguished desperation in Simon's voice numbing her completely.

'I have to, Simon. You know that.' Lisa's voice was low and muffled, her back rigid. 'If I stay...I don't want an affair with you...I couldn't do that to Clemmy.'

'I don't want an *affair* with you, Lissy. I love you...'

She couldn't be hearing this. Would wake up any moment and find it was a nightmare. The numbness had eased, the first wash of agonising pain tearing through Clemency. This could not be happening, not to her. She wanted to cry out her protest, her denial as she watched her husband cross the floor and take her best friend in his arms but her throat was too raw.

'Lissy, please.'

'No, Simon...' Pushing him away, Lisa swung back to the window. 'I love you, but I love Clemmy too. I've known her since I was five, even longer than you have. She's like a sister.' Her voice was so low, Clemency could barely distinguish the words. 'I couldn't ruin her life, and nor could you, Simon.'

They already had...

Her eyes flicking open, Clemency stretched out her stiffening legs and leant back against the tree. Perhaps if she'd tackled Simon and Lisa right then it might have been easier, less painful in the long run. But she hadn't. She'd turned and crept away like a wounded animal, grabbed her coat and escaped silently out of the flat into the December night.

Oblivious to the squeal of taxi brakes, moving like a sleepwalker, Clemency crossed the road to the river embankment. For a moment she stared down into the dark, cold water and then began walking along its edge, her pace increasing until she was almost running. Head bowed, her eyes blurred with unshed tears, she didn't see the group of young men approaching until it was too late to take evasive action and almost cannoned straight into them.

'Happy New Year, beautiful.'

'What's a woman like you doing on her own tonight?'

'Fancy coming to a party with us, gorgeous?'

Their bantering was good-humoured—if puerile— rather than threatening, and normally Clemency wouldn't have had any trouble in dealing with the group of intoxicated but harmless young men. But tonight she simply stared dazedly at the group forming a half-circle around her.

'Scram!'

The deep, educated voice came from behind her. Quiet and controlled, it held an authority that was immediately recognised and acted upon. Macho bravado evaporating, the young men dissolved into sheepish small boys, murmuring apologies to Clemency before hastening on their way.

'Are you all right?'

Tilting her head, Clemency looked up at the tall, quietly spoken man.

'Yes, I'm fine,' she said mechanically. The glow of the street lights illuminated strongly carved male features.

'Where are you going? It might be advisable to take a taxi.'

It was the flicker of concern in the dark, shadowed eyes, the gentleness in the deep voice that proved to be her undoing. 'I d-don't know where I'm going,' she mumbled in a small, bewildered voice and burst into tears.

Vaguely she was aware of a firm hand on her arm propelling her towards a bench. He made no attempt to assuage her tears, offered no trite words of comfort, simply sat there silently by her side, letting her cry without question or intrusion. Yet his very presence, his aura of calm strength was more soothing than a million platitudes.

Her tears subsiding, she dabbed at her cheeks with a tissue and turned towards him. She had never broken down in front of anyone in her life before, should have felt self-conscious and awkward, but she felt neither. Maybe it was because he himself showed no signs of embarrassment or impatience, the corners of the very masculine mouth curving in a reassuring smile, the dark blue eyes inviting but not pressing her to tell him the cause of her distress.

There were tiny laughter lines etched on his face, hinting at a strong sense of humour, a sense of the absurd. A man not given to small talk but, she suspected from the astute eyes, an acute observer. His clean-shaven jaw was lean, well defined, its decisiveness reflected in the square, tenacious chin. In his early thirties, he looked resourceful and competent, not a man to be fazed easily, and certainly not by a weeping female.

She ran a hand over her face again and gave him a watery smile. The embankment was deserted but she felt no qualms about sitting alone in the night with him, not the slightest flicker of unease.

'I'm fine now,' she assured him unconvincingly. 'Please don't let me detain you any further,' she added politely.

He didn't answer. Made no effort to move. Just sat there. Waiting.

'I've just found out that my husband has fallen in love with my best friend,' she blurted out, and saw the leap of compassion in his eyes. She swallowed. 'We were at my brother's party and I overheard them talking in the kitchen...' Jerkily she relived again out loud the most traumatic seconds of her young life. 'I just ran away,' she concluded in a mumble.

'You had no idea?' the man beside her asked softly.

'No. Not a clue. I thought we were happy,' she said bleakly. 'I've known Simon since I was at primary school. He was my first boyfriend when I was sixteen.' She paused, her luminous eyes huge with pain and bewilderment. 'How can you know someone almost all your life, live with them, share their bed and not really know anything about them at all? Not really know what they're thinking, feeling?'

'I don't know.'

His voice was even but the muscle flickering along the lean jaw betrayed him, alerted Clemency immediately. He wasn't simply paying lip service to the words but actually understood—no, more than that—shared her dazed incredulity.

Slowly she searched his face, her eyes locking with his. And for the first time she saw the unhappiness in the dark blue depths. He wasn't as she'd automatically supposed *en route* to a party, but, like her, had deliberately sought out the solitude and anonymity of the river embankment. This man was suffering as much as she was.

Her heart squeezed, aching for him, her own pain momentarily forgotten as she silently willed him to confide in her as she had in him. She saw the hesitancy on his face, the hesitancy of a man accustomed to keeping his own counsel, dealing with his own problems.

Then she saw the doubt disappear and was aware of a sudden jolt of warmth at the knowledge that he trusted her as instinctively as she did him. Why it should matter so much that he did so, when her whole life was falling apart, was too confusing even to think about.

'I found out this afternoon that my wife's pregnant,' he said quietly.

Clemency looked up at him uncomprehendingly. Surely that was cause for celebration, wasn't it?

'She's known for six weeks.'

'Six weeks?' she echoed. How could his wife have kept the news to herself for six weeks? Not wanted to share it with him immediately?

'She doesn't want the baby,' he said abruptly. 'She doesn't want our child. My child.'

The pain in his voice cut through Clemency like a knife, driving everything else from her mind.

'Laura's an interior designer. A very successful one.

She's just won a prestigious overseas contract which she's due to start in June next year.'

By which time she would be nearing the end of her unplanned and unwanted pregnancy.

The chiselled mouth twisted. 'Lousy timing, hmm?' He paused. 'I always knew that Laura's career was important to her.' His voice was so low that Clemency had to strain her ears to hear it. 'But I didn't realise...'

That it was the most important part of her life, more important than her husband or their unborn child. The unspoken words hung in the air, the raw, naked hurt etched on his face almost unbearable. Knowing just how inadequate any words she could offer would be, Clemency reacted instinctively. Inhibitions abandoned in the overwhelming need to comfort him, she reached out and gently took hold of his hand.

His strong, lean fingers tightened around her small palm and then slowly relaxed but didn't release their hold. The tension easing from his face, he smiled down at her wryly.

She smiled back, a sense of complete unreality engulfing her, the blue eyes anaesthetising her to everything but the sensations induced by the warm male fingers folded lightly around hers. She was sitting in the dark on a London bench holding hands with a man whose name she didn't even know and yet it felt the most natural thing in the world to be doing, as if, far from being strangers, they were old, familiar friends. *Or lovers.*

She stiffened, horrified at the insidious thought, further appalled to realise that Simon had completely slipped from the forefront of her mind. Oh, God, Simon and Lisa. She began to shudder as reality crashed over her again.

'You're getting cold.'

She nodded, the protectiveness and concern in the deep voice making her throat constrict with the effort of keeping back another flood of tears. How could this man's wife not want his child? How could anyone hurt him like this? It took every ounce of control not to launch herself into his arms, hold him, hug him.

'I'll walk you back,' he said quietly, pulling her gently to her feet.

She nodded again, both relieved and bereft as he released her hand. Shortening his strides to match hers, he accompanied her as she retraced her path along the river bank towards her brother's flat, the silence between them no longer comfortable but increasingly constrained. Clemency ground to a halt, indicating the illuminated three-storey house across the road, the sound of music spilling out into the night from the ground-floor flat.

'It's just over there.' As she spoke the music was abruptly silenced, raised voices beginning a countdown. Ten, nine...

Eight seconds to midnight. Clemency stared up at the house. Was Simon standing beside Lisa? Had he even noticed she was missing or was he too lost in his own misery even to care?

'One...' As the exuberant voices reached a crescendo, she turned to look up at the figure towering by her side, his dark face as strained as her own.

'Happy New Year,' she murmured wryly, and felt an inane bubble of laughter rising in her throat, the words so hopelessly inappropriate under the circumstances.

'Happy New Year,' he returned, and she saw his own

mouth quirk as he too recognised the absurdity of their seasonal exchange. His eyes moved slowly over her face. 'Take care, hmm?'

'You too,' Clemency said unsteadily. Once this man turned and walked away she would never see him again. The tightness in her chest had nothing to do with Simon.

Impulsively she stood up on tiptoe, intending to plant a swift, chaste kiss on his cheek. Simultaneously he lowered his head to bestow a similar parting gesture, but as she unexpectedly tilted her face upwards his mouth, instead of grazing her forehead, closed over her lips.

The warm, firm mouth barely brushed hers and yet it acted like a touch paper, heat instantly pooling in the pit of her stomach, flaring up, gathering momentum, scorching through her veins. She heard his sharp intake of breath as he lifted his head, his dark face rigid with shock.

For a second she could hardly breathe, let alone think, stared up at him with wide, stunned eyes, drawing desperate gulps of air into her burning lungs. Then she turned and ran.

With a tiny, convulsive shiver, Clemency jerked herself to her feet and paced across the garden, coming to a standstill by the wooden fence that separated her garden from the open farmland beyond.

More than five years on and she could still remember that mindless panic with which she'd fled Joshua Harrington that night. Her hands tightened over the fence and then relaxed. She'd been in a total daze that night, emotionally completely off-balance, vulnerable to anyone who'd shown a modicum of sympathy and understanding.

Turning around, she began to make her way briskly up the garden and faltered, her eyes drawn like a magnet to the red-tiled roof adjacent to her own. Why of all people did her new neighbour have to be him? She'd made a new life for herself with which she was perfectly content.

· Oh, for heaven's sake, Clemency. She pulled herself up irritably. There was no earthly reason why her orderly existence should be remotely affected by her new neighbour. Joshua Harrington, she reminded herself firmly, had made it perfectly clear that he had no intention of intruding into her life, let alone changing it.

CHAPTER THREE

MUFFLING a yawn, Clemency zipped up her jeans and tugged a green cotton sweater over her rumpled red curls. Barefoot, she padded across to her bedroom window and flung it open, surveying the cloudless blue sky. It looked as if it was going to be another glorious day.

Yawning again, she slipped on her sandals and made her way downstairs. She bent to retrieve the newspaper and mail from the front doormat and headed down the hall, coming to an abrupt halt as she heard the sound of breaking glass.

One of the cats from the local farm knocking down a milk bottle? Except she didn't keep her empty bottles outside her back door. She took a tentative step forward and froze. Someone was breaking into her kitchen...

'Please, Daddy, let me do it.'

'Sorry, old chap. Back you go. You too, Tommy, please.'

She expelled a long, deep breath. Did prospective burglars normally bring their four-year-old sons along as witnesses? Tiptoeing to the door, she stealthily eased it open a crack and peeped through.

Armed with gloves and a small hammer, Joshua Harrington was casually knocking out the glass in her open back door onto a plastic sheet. From the safety of the lawn, the twins, identically dressed today in the brown uniform of the village school, watched with expressions of utter longing on their small faces.

Clemency's eyes dropped to the football at their feet and her eyes darkened reflectively. One hell of a kick for such small legs—over the hedge with still enough force to smash her window.

Pushing open the door, she stepped into the kitchen.

'Good morning,' she said breezily.

If she'd hoped to throw Joshua Harrington even marginally off-balance, she was disappointed.

'I thought you'd be at work by now,' he murmured mildly, the navy blue sweatshirt hugging the wide, powerful shoulders intensifying the brilliance of his eyes. Knocking out the last fragment of glass, he stooped to gather up the plastic sheeting.

Normally she would have been, Clemency conceded, but it wouldn't have hurt him to ring the doorbell and check. 'I'm on leave for a week.'

Waggling her fingers at the twins, who were waving to her enthusiastically from the garden, Clemency retrieved the strong refuse bag from the floor and held it open.

'Thanks.'

As he deposited the plastic sheeting deftly into the bag, her eyes flicked over the strong contours of his face, absorbing the weariness etched into it. For a second her hard-won composure almost cracked completely, the muscles of her stomach coiling into a fierce knot. Had he endured an equally troubled night? Lain awake for hours, like her, eyes open, staring into the past?

'Daddy's going to put a lovely new window in your door,' trebled a small voice. Evidently deciding that their temporary banishment had been lifted now the glass had been safely removed, the twins scampered across the grass.

'That's really kind of him, isn't it?' The second voice piped, with unconcealed hero-worship.

'Yes, it certainly is,' Clemency agreed solemnly, her muscles relaxing as the small boys bounded into the kitchen.

'Especially as Daddy broke the damn window,' Joshua Harrington murmured *sotto voce*, the corners of the firm, straight mouth twitching.

Unable to keep it straight any longer, Clemency's face broke into a warm, wide grin, the wariness in her eyes of which she'd been quite unconscious clearing briefly.

'Where's your lunch box, Tommy?' Joshua enquired, straightening up.

'Left it in the garden.'

'Go and fetch it, please.'

'Yes, Daddy.' The boys started for the door and then, as if some invisible hand had tapped them on the shoulder, turned back towards Clemency.

'Bye, Clemency,' they chorused dutifully.

'An' thank you for having us...' one voice continued absently, parrot fashion.

'You don't have to say that...' Its owner was instantly corrected.

'Goodbye, Jamie,' Clemency said formally, repressing her laughter, a little mystified at the expression of utter resignation on their small faces as they looked up at her. They were so adorable, she could hug them! 'Goodbye, Tommy.'

For a second neither of them moved and then, faces lighting up with relief, they turned and bounded towards the door.

'She didn't kiss us...' The clear, carrying voice floated jubilantly back through the open door.

'Or hug us...'

'I believe,' Joshua Harrington murmured dryly, 'that you've just passed the litmus test.'

Clemency couldn't quite meet his eyes. She so very nearly hadn't!

'An' she smelled nice...'

'Even nicer than Anna.'

Anna again, Clemency mused; but on that tantalising note the small voices faded away.

'Hmm.' Joshua gathered up the refuse bag and headed for the door. 'I think I might have a word with my sons and heirs about the importance of discretion,' he murmured thoughtfully.

'Do as I say, not as I do?' Clemency enquired innocently before she could help herself.

'How much of my diatribe *did* you overhear yesterday?'

'You mean did I hear the "to hell with all women" soliloquy?'

'Or the reference to the inquisitive, frustrated spinster next door?'

'I don't think those were quite my words...' he refuted, his mouth quirking.

'No,' she conceded, 'but that was the inference,' she continued lightly. 'The implication that no woman could possibly feel fulfilled without the presence of a man in her life. An arrogant male assumption that isn't true.' She smiled back at him to take the sting out of her words, to show him she was half-teasing. Nevertheless, it suddenly seemed very important to assure him, however obliquely, that she had absolutely no designs on either him or the twins, wasn't in the market for happy families.

She saw his eyes flicker, but their expression was as unreadable as his face.

'The assumption works both ways,' he drawled. 'I've had my fill over the past few years of the manipulative attempts at matchmaking by the wives of various male acquaintances.'

His voice was as light and as casual as hers had been, but perversely the underlying tension between them seemed to intensify rather than ease. They were making ground rules, Clemency absorbed, warning each other off—though why it should be necessary to do so was something she didn't care to analyse.

'I'll pick up a pane of glass after I've dropped the boys off at school.' Glancing at his watch, he grimaced slightly, and hurried outside to herd up his sons, their small, bowed heads on a level just above his knees as they scampered by his side, trying to keep pace with his long, rapid strides.

Moving across to the window, Clemency watched the tall, lean, assured figure disappear around the side of the house, her grey eyes thoughtful. She had nothing but admiration for those courageous women who had attempted to interfere in his private life. And she very much doubted that Joshua Harrington had ever been manipulated by anyone in his entire existence.

Breakfast! Turning away from the window, Clemency moved across the tiled floor, extracted a loaf of bread from the fridge and, changing her mind, replaced it. She'd skip her usual tea and toast this morning, settle for a cup of instant coffee instead. Her mouth twitched. Live dangerously, change her routine!

Switching on the kettle, she picked up the newspaper while she waited for the water to boil, her gaze darting immediately to the cartoon at the bottom of the front page. Josh. The distinctive, decisive signature was oddly redolent of its owner, instantly conjuring up an image of the dark, rugged face.

Abruptly she tossed the paper to one side, the cartoon for some reason failing to amuse her this morning, and armed with a mug of coffee sat down at the breakfast bar. She glanced up at the wall clock. How long would it take him to drop the twins off and buy a new pane of glass?

Determinedly she turned her attention to her post. Mostly junk mail. An exceedingly rude postcard from David Mason. Idiot. She smiled, thinking affectionately of the russet-haired man who had somehow managed the difficult task of maintaining his friendship with both herself and Simon.

Her smile faded. Had David known about Simon's feelings for Lisa all those years ago? Let himself be used as an alibi on occasions? Had those games of squash with Simon been fictitious? She winced. Oh, blast Joshua Harrington. He was the one indirectly responsible for reviving those painful questions, questions she had resolutely dismissed years ago.

Slipping off her stool, she carried her mug of coffee through to the sitting room at the front of the house. Was that the sound of his car now? Tensing, she gazed out of the window into the lane. No, just a tractor *en route* to the farm. Restlessly she wandered back to the kitchen, had just sat down again when the doorbell chimed.

Trying to ignore the rush of adrenalin spurting through her, she jumped to her feet and went to answer it. Joshua had evidently decided to announce his arrival more formally this time.

Taking a deep breath, she opened the door expectantly, perturbed by the immediate sense of anticlimax as she saw the grey-haired man standing in front of her. Recovering quickly, her mouth curved in a warm, welcoming smile.

'Hello, William.'

His gnarled, weather-beaten face creased in a beam. 'Brought you something for your supper tonight,' he said laconically and without preamble. Digging into the pocket of the voluminous waxed jacket that he wore both summer and winter, and, Clemency sometimes suspected, even to bed, he drew out a brown paper parcel and thrust it into her hands. 'Fresh this morning.'

'Oh, how lovely!' Clemency exclaimed enthusiastically, her heart dropping as she felt the clammy contents through the paper. 'I shall look forward to them.' Stooping down, she petted the black and white collie sitting obediently by the gum-booted feet. 'Thank you very much.' She smiled, straightening up, only then noticing the lean figure coming up the drive towards them.

'Come on, Jesse.' Nodding his head with satisfaction at Clemency's evident pleasure with his gift, the elderly countryman made his way back down the drive, returning Joshua's courteous greeting as they passed with a monosyllabic grunt.

'A man of few words,' Joshua commented as, a tool box in one hand, a pane of glass in the other, he reached Clemency's side.

'William doesn't say a lot,' Clemency conceded, trying to ignore the way the sun's rays were flickering over the thick, rich dark hair, caressing the hard contours of his face. 'But he and his wife are very sweet,' she added over her shoulder, leading Joshua down the hall and into the kitchen. She was unsuccessful in camouflaging her slight shudder as she deposited the package on the sink unit, and sighed resignedly as she met the quizzical blue gaze.

'They don't have a car any more so I give them the occasional lift into Bournemouth,' she said vaguely. She didn't mention the fortnight last winter when she'd faithfully driven William over to the hospital every evening to visit his wife who'd been recovering after a fall.

'And William and his wife express their appreciation with mysterious brown parcels?' Depositing his tool box and the pane of glass on the floor, Joshua's eyes dropped thoughtfully back to the sink unit.

'William was a gamekeeper until he retired.' Clemency's own eyes returned to the package. Oh, heavens, it hadn't moved had it? No, that was definitely her imagination. 'And I suppose he still has, um, contacts in that line.' She had never enquired too closely about the source of her presents. 'It's usually fish, like today. But sometimes it's a rabbit or even a pheasant.' Her large, expressive eyes darkened unhappily. 'William just assumes that I can...prepare them.' She paused and confessed in a guilty rush, 'I know it's dreadful but I bury them at the bottom of the garden.'

'In the dead of night so no one can see you?' The corners of his mouth twitching, Joshua turned his attention to the back door.

'It's not funny,' Clemency reproved, but she grinned back at him and then sighed. 'I should have been honest with William right from the start.' Leaning back against the sink unit, she watched as Joshua deftly inserted the new pane of glass into the door, fascinated by his dexterity. 'And told him I was just a feeble, squeamish townie.' She'd held one of those strong, capable hands, felt the warmth of those long, supple fingers against hers. She swallowed hard. 'Or claimed to be a strict vegetarian, but...'

Her stomach muscles contracted in a fierce knot as against her will her eyes skidded over the chiselled mouth. Why did she have to start remembering *that kiss* now? Just when she'd begun to feel at ease with him, begun to relax.

Taking a step backwards, Joshua examined his handiwork and, apparently satisfied, glanced back over his shoulder. 'I picked up a couple of new bolts while I was out.' Discarding his sweatshirt, he tossed it casually over a chair, the tanned length of his arms sprinkled with fine, dark hairs revealed by the dark blue T-shirt.

Clemency felt herself stiffening. She didn't want his unnerving masculine presence in her home for one moment longer than was strictly necessary.

'Thanks.' She forced out the word but knew from the slight narrowing of his eyes he'd noticed her hesitation. But hopefully, she prayed inwardly, not the reason for it. 'I really ought to have changed the old bolts before now,' she added more lightly. Joshua had demonstrated just how easy it was to gain access to her home now the rusty bolts were no longer functional, she admitted. Especially as she did occasionally forget to remove the key from the lock.

Armed with a screwdriver, Joshua dropped to his haunches by the door, the blue denim jeans tautening across the muscular thighs. Clemency averted her gaze abruptly. 'Coffee?' She had to occupy herself with something, couldn't just stand there watching him—or trying not to watch him—any longer.

'Yes, please.' He looked up. 'Black. No sugar.'

'Right.' His eyes under the thick sweep of dark lashes were so impossibly blue, the depth and intensity of the colour almost mesmerising. She turned away swiftly and spooned coffee into two mugs, cursing under her breath as the spoon slid from her fingers and landed on the tiled floor with a resounding clatter. Bending down to retrieve it, she sensed Joshua watching her.

'Yes?' she enquired silently, lifting her eyebrows.

'Nothing.' The innocent blue eyes answered wordlessly. Smiling blandly, he began collecting up his tools.

One black coffee, one white, Clemency reminded herself firmly. Surreptitiously she watched Joshua as he rinsed his hands and drew up a chair to the table. Sitting sideways, he stretched out his long, lean legs indolently in front of him, crooking a muscular arm around the back. This was her house, her kitchen and yet right now he seemed to be the one completely at home, not her, she thought with a prickle of resentment.

Picking up the mugs carefully, she carried them across to the table and handed him one.

'Thanks.'

Sitting down opposite him, she took a sip of coffee and flicked him an upward glance. The dark blue eyes were resting pensively on her left hand, the betraying band of white skin on her third finger long since disappeared.

'I used to wonder occasionally what had happened to you. How everything had turned out.'

The quiet admission was so unexpected it made Clemency start.

'Did you?' she said with studied casualness, wondering why she found it so difficult—no, impossible—to make the same admission. 'Simon and I separated when I moved down here four and a half years ago,' she said instead, after a pause. 'We've been divorced for two.' She wasn't unduly surprised by his slight frown as he registered the time discrepancy.

'I didn't confront Simon about Lisa straight away,' she said evenly, and saw the furrow between the dark eyebrows deepen.

'Why not?' he said quietly.

She averted her eyes. *Initially because I felt so damn guilty about you.* It had been absolutely absurd in retrospect, particularly under the circumstances. One fleeting New Year kiss—and for a while she'd actually felt as guilty about Simon as if she'd been the betrayer not the betrayed. She'd waited nearly five weeks before finally confronting Simon.

'I suppose I convinced myself that he was simply infatuated with Lisa, that once she went to America he would forget her. It wasn't as if he'd actually had an affair with her, been physically unfaithful.' Was that really true or had she simply chosen to believe it? Put her own interpretation on the words she'd overheard in the kitchen?

'And then when you finally did tackle Simon about Lisa?' Joshua asked quietly.

Clemency studied the table. Simon's distress at the pain he'd caused her had been almost as unbearable as her own hurt. 'We decided to give our marriage another shot.' For nine long months they'd tried so hard, both concealing their increasing unhappiness beneath a veneer of superficial domestic normality. 'It didn't work out. Simon didn't stop loving Lisa just because she went to America, and I stopped deluding myself that he had.'

Her eyes darkened, remembering both the sadness and relief with which she and Simon had finally agreed that their marriage was over. A marriage, she had gradually come to realise, that should never have taken place. Simon hadn't fallen out of love with her—he'd never been in love with her in the first place. A deep affection, a loyalty grown out of a shared childhood had never been a strong enough basis for a lifelong commitment as man and wife. They had been friends but never truly lovers.

'Simon and Lisa were married six months ago,' she finished steadily. It was completely irrational but it had still hurt.

'A happy ending for Simon.' The blue eyes moved over her face. 'And you, Clemency? Are you happy?' he enquired softly.

Was she? 'I like living on my own,' she said slowly, occurring to her only then just how much she did value her independence, just how reluctant she would be to give it up. Okay she did get lonely occasionally, but that was a small price to pay for the advantages of her single status. Never again would her personal happiness be reliant on someone else.

'And you enjoy your job?' He lifted a quizzical eyebrow.

'Yes, I do,' she acknowledged, and frowned, not wholly comfortable with the image she was presenting of a self-sufficient, independent career woman. Well, it was an apt one, wasn't it? This was the second time in as many days that Joshua Harrington had triggered off this introspection, stirred up some tiny core of dissatisfaction within her, she realised uneasily.

'At least my career is proving to be more rewarding and fulfilling than my marriage,' she said with a rare touch of bitterness, and could have bitten off her tongue as she saw the shutters slam down over the blue eyes.

'A view apparently shared by my ex-wife,' he observed caustically.

How could she have been so unbelievably thoughtless? Clemency opened her mouth and closed it again, knowing that to start apologising would only compound her gaffe. Unhappily she watched as he took a sip of coffee, her gaze moving over the hard features, the cynicism once again pronounced.

'Laura resented her pregnancy for its entire duration.' He raised his head abruptly. 'She returned to work full-time almost immediately the twins were born, leaving them in charge of a nanny. As her reputation grew, she spent more and more time travelling overseas. Our home became little more than her base in England. On the occasions she was at home, we were like strangers, sharing nothing but the same roof.'

Clemency's eyes didn't waver from his face. His voice was even, devoid of all emotion, but it was all too easy to fill in the gaps left by the skeleton account of the disintegration of his marriage.

'Prolonging the marriage for the sake of the children hardly seemed appropriate under the circumstances. In fact,' he said wryly, 'I think Laura saw more of the boys once we were separated. They used to think it was a great adventure, going to stay the night at her flat.'

Past tense, Clemency registered.

'We were divorced eighteen months ago and Laura

now lives in the States. She sees the boys whenever she comes to England, phones them, never forgets their birthday.' He paused. 'In her own way, I think she does care about them.'

'Do the twins miss her?'

'They did a little at first but they rarely mention her now, seem to have accepted the situation quite easily, though no doubt when they're older they'll start asking more questions.' He shrugged. 'I don't think Laura was ever a large enough part of their lives for them to really feel the loss. In fact they were far more upset when Sue, their nanny, left a year ago. Unfortunately due to a family crisis she had to leave very suddenly, giving them no time to get used to the idea.' He paused. 'I didn't replace Sue with another full-time nanny.'

Clemency nodded. He hadn't wanted to run the risk of the twins becoming attached to yet another woman who might disappear from their lives. That Tommy and Jamie appeared to be such happy, well-adjusted small boys despite the two emotional upheavals in their short lives was in no small way attributable to their father, she conceded thoughtfully.

Her eyes moved speculatively over the strong face. Had the ban on women been applied just as rigorously to his own life? It was difficult to believe that he'd been completely devoid of feminine company since his divorce, though his evident determination not to allow anyone into his domestic life must have placed severe limitations on any relationship.

'Can I get off the couch now?' the deep voice enquired dryly.

'Sorry?' Clemency blinked at him innocently. 'Miles

away,' she murmured airily, starting to rise to her feet automatically as she heard the doorbell ring.

'Don't get up,' Joshua drawled, unfurling his long frame with deceptive speed from his chair. 'It'll probably be for me.'

To her disbelief Clemency found herself instantly obeying the commanding hand as it waved her back to her seat. He was giving her orders in her own home now?

'I'm expecting some fencing this morning, and left a note explaining where I was,' he added casually, striding into the hall. 'Thanks for the coffee.'

There was the murmur of male voices followed a few seconds later by the slam of her front door.

Well, really! Clemency felt a gurgle of laughter rising in her throat as she surveyed the chair opposite her. She had wished for his departure, but hadn't expected it to be quite so abrupt.

Permission to stand up in my own house? She inclined her head towards the empty chair and, gathering up the two empty mugs, carried them across to the sink, heaving a sigh as her eyes encountered the brown parcel.

Don't be a wimp, Clemency Adams, she admonished herself and, taking a deep breath, unwrapped the parcel and placed the contents in a bowl. You're living in the country now. Gritting her teeth, she retrieved a sharp knife from a drawer and then let it slip through her hands onto the counter.

'Okay, I'm a wimp,' she muttered out loud. 'If a tiny little field mouse walked through the door, I'd probably leap on a chair. So what? I *enjoy* being a wimp. I've no desire to learn to ride so what does it matter if horses terrify me too? Come to think of it I'm not over-keen on some of those enormous cows that graze in the field beyond the bottom of the garden.'

'But, other than that, you're a country girl at heart?'

Slowly Clemency turned round in the direction of the deep, mocking voice and saw the lean figure standing on the threshold of the back door.

'Don't you ever knock?' Clemency demanded, the laughing blue eyes making her stomach turn an involuntary somersault 'I was having a private conversation,' she informed him with great dignity.

'Forgot my tool box,' he drawled laconically, the amusement in the blue eyes intensifying as, ignoring her rhetorical question, he sauntered across to her side.

'Mmm. Trout,' he murmured appreciatively, looking in the bowl.

'You want them, they're yours,' Clemency offered with benevolent grandeur, trying to ignore just how close she was to that six-foot mass of solid male muscle.

'Thanks.'

He never wasted time with banalities, never prevaricated, Clemency mused, watching as he unhesitatingly wrapped up the fish and picked them up, his actions and words always direct and positive.

'I promised the boys we'd have a barbecue tonight.'

'Barbecued trout?' Clemency queried doubtfully, though on reflection she realised it would be much the same as grilling them.

'My speciality,' he informed her modestly, retrieving his tool kit. He paused in the open doorway. 'If you feel like it later, come on round and join us. Sixish.'

Clemency blinked. Was he actually issuing an invitation into that all-male preserve?

'Right, thanks. I might just do that,' she returned with

equal casualness, deliberately not committing herself to a firm acceptance. 'Oh, don't forget your sweatshirt...' She picked it up from the chair where he'd strewn it earlier and darted out the back door. Too late. He'd gone.

She turned back into the kitchen. The scent of clean, soapy male skin clung to the sweatshirt, teased her sense of smell, the fragrance a disturbing, evocative reminder of its owner. Swiftly she tossed the sweatshirt back over a chair. She would take it around with her tonight—if she decided to go.

CHAPTER FOUR

SO DID she take it with her or not? Her hair still damp from the tepid shower, Clemency fastened the zip of her olive-green shorts as she considered the bottle of wine cooling in her fridge downstairs. If it had been anyone else but Joshua she wouldn't have even hesitated, would have taken the bottle as a matter of course. But the thought of presenting it to Joshua to share *à deux* was one from which she shied away.

She pulled a white V-necked T-shirt over her head and walked over to her open bedroom window, grateful for the gentle evening breeze after the heat of the day. Better to take something the twins could enjoy too— such as the early strawberries she'd picked up from a farm shop that afternoon.

She grinned wryly. She was taking a casual invitation from a neighbour to a family barbecue a little too seriously. Of course she didn't even have to go, hadn't given a firm acceptance.

She slipped on her sandals and frowned, the thought of spending a solitary evening unappealing. She'd had enough of her own company for one day, she admitted uneasily.

Soon after Joshua had left that morning, she'd packed up a picnic, sun block and a hat and had headed for the coast, taking the ferry from Poole over to Studland, walking along the cliff path to the small seaside town of Swanage.

It was a walk she'd undertaken several times before but today for some reason as she'd sat eating her picnic from her favourite vantage point on top of the headland, gazing out across the bay, listening to the waves crashing against the weathered rocks below her, instead of the usual feeling of tranquil contentment, she'd felt an inexplicable restlessness, a tiny core of emptiness gnawing inside her. She'd returned home tired but without the sense of exhilaration that normally accompanied a day of strenuous exercise and fresh air.

The sound of clear, piping voices followed by gurgles of laughter carried on the breeze into her room, the laughter so infectious she found herself grinning in response, her mood instantly lifting. Galvanised into action, she ran a comb through her tumble of red curls and made her way downstairs.

It wasn't until she was pressing Joshua's doorbell some minutes later that she remembered she'd forgotten his sweatshirt, instantly forgetting it again as the towering figure appeared from around the side of the house. Faded denims slung low over his lean hips, short-sleeved blue shirt fitted across the width of his shoulders, he was dressed as casually as he had been that morning. But there was nothing remotely casual about Clemency's immediate and wholly feminine response to him, the dryness in her mouth as she acknowledged the sheer force of his rugged male attractiveness.

'Hello.' He greeted her with easy assurance, his teeth very white against his tanned skin.

Her returning smile was unnatural, forced, and with it came the terrible compulsion to turn round and go home. Flee from him as she had on that New Year's Eve five years ago? a treacherous little voice taunted her.

'Come on through.'

She started, realising that he was holding the side gate open for her.

'Thank you.' She was aware of just how ridiculously stiff and formal she sounded, aware too of the thoughtful eyes moving fleetingly over her face as he ushered her around to the back garden, a tantalising but unrecognisable smell issuing from the barbecue set in the middle of the lawn.

'Home-made vegeburgers,' Joshua enlightened her as they walked towards it. 'My mother makes them for the boys.'

'Hello, Clemency.' A small figure clad in a green T-shirt and blue shorts rushed across the lawn towards them. 'I think they need turning over, Daddy.' He hopped up and down by their side. 'Can I do it? Please, Daddy? I know how to and I'll be very careful.'

'No, Jamie,' Joshua said firmly, ruffling the dark head. 'Now, go and wash your hands please.'

'Yes, Daddy,' Jamie answered resignedly and paused, eyeing the covered plastic carton in Clemency's hand with unconcealed curiosity. Obligingly she opened the lid and let him peep in.

'Strawberries,' he whooped with delight. 'They're my favouritest.' Giving his father no time to correct his grammar, he tore off into the house.

'Glass of wine?' Joshua invited, picking up an opened bottle from the trestle table placed beside the barbecue.

'Thanks,' Clemency nodded. Placing the strawberries next to the large covered bowl of enticing-looking salad, Clemency's eyes settled on the small boy sitting cross-legged on the grass. Striped T-shirt, she noted mentally.

Oblivious to everything around him, he was staring down intently at the palm of his hand.

'Ladybird,' Joshua drawled casually, following her gaze. 'He's waiting for it to fly away home.'

'Oh.' She looked at him blankly for a second and then the vague recollection of the childhood ditty stirred in her memory. 'Yes, of course,' she said lamely, taking hold of the proffered glass.

'Tommy,' Joshua called out gently. 'Put her on a bush now and go and wash your hands.'

'Yes, Daddy.' Tommy looked up gravely. 'Hello, Clemency.' Slowly and carefully he rose to his feet, took a step forward and stopped. 'She's gone,' he announced sadly, studying his empty palm, and then, dropping to all fours, scampered towards the house, miaowing vociferously.

Startled, Clemency looked at Joshua.

'Thomas is desperate for a cat and this is his idea of subtlety,' he informed her dryly as he moved to the barbecue and deftly flipped the burgers over with a slice.

Clemency grinned, feeling her tension beginning to ease. Taking a sip of wine, her eyes drifted around the garden. He'd evidently made a start on his fencing today, she observed, noting the new panels at the bottom. No more surprise visitors, she mused a little regretfully.

'Enjoyed the first day of your holiday?' Joshua enquired idly, adding two portions of fish to the sizzling grill.

Not quite as much as she'd anticipated. 'I took the ferry over to Studland,' she answered casually instead, avoiding a direct answer.

'Hence the profusion of freckles.' He smiled.

She smiled back, the warmth suffusing her out of all

proportion to the teasing observation. 'It's one of my favourite places on the coast,' she said lightly, puzzled by the unreadable, fleeting expression in his eyes.

'The twins love the beach there. I used to take them over whenever we visited my parents.'

She jolted. She'd forgotten that his parents lived locally, that he would be familiar with the area. It gave her the strangest sensation to know how close he must have been geographically at times over the past four-odd years. She'd visited the same sandy beach as him on numerous occasions, both during the summer and winter. And on any one of those occasions she might have seen a tall, dark-haired man with two small boys walking across the shell-strewn sand towards her. It would have been too much of a coincidence; she dismissed the disturbing image unfurling in her head swiftly. An even greater coincidence than him buying the house next door to her?

'Daddy, they're *burning*...'

Biting back his muffled curse, Joshua swiftly rescued the burgers and fish, deftly inserting the former into rolls for the twins and adding salad.

'Go easy on the tomato sauce,' he warned them briskly as he handed each of them a laden plate. He quirked a dark eyebrow at Clemency. 'I assume that you like your trout well done?' he drawled airily, the implication being that there would be something seriously amiss with her if she didn't prefer it charred around the edges. He grinned. 'Help yourself to salad. I said easy on the ketchup, Jamie!'

Swept along in the sudden flurry of activity, Clemency found herself seated on a slatted wooden seat beside

Tommy, his twin having elected to sit on a rug beside his father.

'Cats like fish,' Tommy informed her gravely, studying her plate.

'Want to try a bit?' Clemency offered.

'You can have a piece of my burger.'

Exchanging smiles, they traded and sampled in silence.

'Nice,' Tommy commented thoughtfully after a few moments' contemplation.

Clemency nodded in agreement, swallowing her morsel of vegeburger. How could you still be so aware of someone when all your senses were fully occupied elsewhere? She forced herself to concentrate on her plate for a few more moments and then, unable to resist any longer, her eyes flicked across to the rug, her mouth instantly curving in an involuntary grin.

His posture identical to his father's—back upright, small legs stretched out, ankles crossed—Jamie was keeping a determinedly vigilant eye on Joshua, faithfully shadowing his slightest move. As Joshua put down his knife and fork and drained his glass, Jamie hastily dropped his burger onto his plate and picked up his beaker of orange squash.

'How's the fish?' The suppressed amusement in Joshua's eyes as he glanced up echoed her own, their fleeting conspiratorial exchange sending a tingle down her spine.

'Nice and crunchy,' she teased, and then added honestly, 'It's delicious.' It was delicately flavoured with almonds; he'd evidently brushed it with some sort of coating before grilling it. 'How did you make the sauce?' she asked with genuine interest.

'An old family recipe,' he said nonchalantly.

'Out of a packet?' she smiled sweetly; his answering grin made her heart dip as if it were on a rollercoaster. 'You must let me have the label,' she said dryly.

'More wine?' His grin widened.

Deciding that she felt sufficiently light-headed, Clemency started to decline but her words were drowned by a loud wail.

'I'm sorry.' Crestfallen, Tommy looked down at his upturned beaker, the contents of which were trickling down Clemency's leg.

'That's all right,' she said peacefully, picking up her paper serviette.

'I didn't mean to...'

'It was just an accident.' Clemency smiled reassuringly, her smile stiffening as she saw the direction of Joshua's gaze, the masculine eyes instinctively following the movement of her hand as it swept the length of a silky, golden leg.

Abruptly she crumpled up the sticky serviette and placed it jerkily on her empty plate.

'Are you cross?' a small voice beside her enquired unhappily.

'Of course not,' Clemency said quickly, willing her tense muscles to relax as she smiled warmly down into the anxious face.

Seemingly convinced, he smiled back at her. 'I'll show you where there are some snails after tea, if you like,' he offered in a confidential whisper. 'And some caterpillars.'

She very much did not like. 'Thank you,' Clemency whispered back.

'An' I'll show you where...'

'Who's ready for their strawberries?'

Clemency never did discover what her third treat was to be, Tommy, to her relief, being instantly distracted by Joshua.

'Me!' he cried enthusiastically.

'And me!' echoed Jamie, adding helpfully as he heard the faint ringing sound from the house, 'Telephone, Daddy.'

'Would you mind...?' Joshua quirked an apologetic dark eyebrow at Clemency, and strode towards the house.

'Probably Daddy's editor,' Jamie said sagely, and yawned. 'Or Granny,' he mumbled.

'Might be Anna,' Tommy contributed and, rubbing his eyes, slid off the bench and joined his twin on the rug.

That was the third time the mysterious Anna had crept into their conversation, Clemency noted, and, resisting the shameful temptation to delve further, collected up the empty plates. She placed them on the table, set out four dishes and began to distribute the strawberries, flapping a hand to ward off a marauding wasp.

'Do you like them mashed up or whole?' Frowning at the complete silence which greeted the enquiry, she glanced over her shoulder.

Tommy and Jamie had collapsed on the rug like two small, exhausted puppies, both sound asleep. Quietly she walked across to the rug, her mouth curving softly as she gazed down at them. They looked so small and vulnerable, so completely defenceless. Bright and articulate, it was easy to forget that they were really little more than babies. Startled by the fierce surge of protectiveness that swept over her, she knelt down and very gently brushed back an errant lock of dark hair from Jamie's forehead, scrambling to her feet self-consciously as she heard the firm footsteps behind her.

'They just crashed out,' she murmured, wondering if she was imagining the slight coolness in the blue eyes. Caught red-handed breaking one of the house rules, she thought wryly; caught giving into a maternal instinct that was far stronger than she'd ever suspected.

'They've only just started going to school full-time.' The unguarded expression on Joshua's face as he looked down at his sons made Clemency's heart twist. No need to wonder about the priority in his life.

Aroused by his father's voice, Jamie stirred, blinking open hazy eyes.

'Come on, old chap,' Joshua said gently. 'Bed-time.'

'I haven't had my strawberries yet,' he mumbled, struggling sleepily to his feet, but the protest was merely a token one.

'Have them tomorrow, hmm?' Scooping up Tommy's recumbent form, Joshua balanced him effortlessly against the crook of his hard shoulder and took hold of Jamie's hand.

'G'night, Clemency.'

'Good night, Jamie.' No hugging, no kissing, she reminded herself sternly.

'Won't be long.'

Feeling oddly excluded, Clemency watched Joshua head towards the house with his small sons, and then, reproving herself mentally for being absurd, she moved briskly back over to the table. Absently popping a strawberry into her mouth, she tipped the remainder back into the plastic container. Might as well make herself useful. Besides, that wasp was beginning to become a nuisance.

Gathering up the used plates, she carried them across the lawn, entering the kitchen by the open back door.

She was in the process of stacking the dishes by the sink when a small pyjama-clad figure burst into the kitchen.

'I can't find Hedgey Bear,' he mumbled fretfully, beginning to hunt feverishly round the room.

'Is this Hedgey Bear?' Clemency asked gently, unearthing an unidentifiable, well-worn furry object from under a pile of papers. It bore no resemblance to a hedgehog, a bear, or any other member of the animal kingdom that she could think of, but, judging by the immediate smile of delight, it was the beloved toy in question.

'Have you found him, Jamie?' Joshua's voice echoed down the hall.

'Yes, Daddy.' Catching her by surprise, Jamie gave Clemency a swift hug around the waist and scurried out of the door.

Smiling, Clemency finished stacking the dishes, her ears alert for the sound of firm footsteps in the hall. Spotting the crumpled serviette that had fallen under the table, she knelt down to retrieve it and yelped out loud, the excruciating pain in her hand out of all proportion to the size of the yellow and black insect that flew past her and out of the door.

Nursing her palm, she rocked to and fro on her heels, her face creased with pain.

'Clemency?'

She jumped at the light touch on her arm, her eyes jerking upwards to see the concerned face bending over her.

'Wasp sting,' she said through gritted teeth.

'Ouch.' The pressure of his hand on her arm increasing, Joshua gently helped her to her feet. 'You're not allergic to them, are you?'

'No.' Not to wasp stings. But she was quite definitely allergic to Joshua Harrington, could already feel herself reacting to his proximity, her stomach muscles contorting into fierce knots, her arm burning from the fleeting touch of his fingers against her bare skin. She wasn't responding to his sympathy, his concern. Her response was nothing to do with Joshua Harrington the person, but everything to do with Joshua Harrington the man.

It took every ounce of will-power not to snatch her hand away as the deft, sure fingers briefly examined her palm.

'Sorry,' he said quietly, evidently, to her relief, misconstruing the reason for her swift intake of breath. Then as she saw the flickering awareness in his eyes realised she'd been wrong, that he was far too astute to have made that error.

Turning away abruptly, he moved across to the first-aid box secured to the wall well out of the twins' reach and extracted a small tube.

'This should soothe it.' He unscrewed the top and handed it to her.

'Thanks.' For one awful moment she'd thought he was planning to administer the antiseptic cream himself. Clumsily, she squeezed out the cream and rubbed it onto her palm, conscious of the blue gaze resting on her averted face.

She flicked him an upward glance, the tube of cream slipping from her rigid figures as she saw the expression in the dark-lashed eyes as they dropped to the curve of her mouth.

'Oh, what the hell...'

She had time to murmur her protest, time to move as he lowered his head but she did neither. With a feeling of inevitability that had been with her since the moment she'd set eyes on him again, Clemency lifted her face up towards him.

There was no slow, escalating feeling of pleasure, just a shuddering sense of relief as his mouth closed over hers in fierce demand. Eyelids flickering downwards, her arms curled up around his neck, her fingers sliding through the thick richness of his hair, relief swiftly changing to a tormenting, driving need as the hard, burning mouth increased its pressure. This was why she'd fled him all those years ago, this was why she'd been so terrified of ever meeting him again. Terrified not of him but herself, of her response to a man she barely knew.

His hands swept down her back, settled on her hips, drawing her into the hard length of his body. No longer capable of coherent thought, she arched against him, her fingers slipping beneath the collar of his shirt, Joshua's swift indrawn breath as intoxicating as the feel of the warm male skin beneath her fingers. She was oblivious to everything but this man, melting into him, tasting him, touching him, drowning in a whirlpool of sensuous pleasure.

'Clemency.'

She mumbled her protest as he lifted his head, swaying dizzily against him, searching for his mouth again.

'Clemency.'

This time the urgency in his voice slowly penetrated through her daze. Unwillingly, her eyelids flickered upwards.

'I want you.' His dilated eyes were almost black.

'I know,' she whispered, hot, melting warmth teasing every inch of her body.

'But if I took you to bed we wouldn't be making love.' Abruptly his hands fell to his side. 'We would be having sex,' he said harshly.

Clemency recoiled both mentally and physically, his words as effective as a physical blow in shocking her back to stark, cold reality. She wanted desperately to tell him that she would never have allowed things to get that far, that it had only been a meaningless kiss, for heaven's sake. But the words wouldn't form on her stiff, swollen lips.

'No strings.' His eyes moved over her face. 'No commitment.'

He didn't have to keep spelling it out as if she were some dewy-eyed, naive, romantic teenager. She hadn't thought for one moment that he felt anything more for her than a transitory physical desire. She winced. For those few insane moments she hadn't been capable of thinking *anything*. Her response to him could hardly be termed cerebral.

'You haven't slept with anyone since Simon, have you?' he said quietly.

It wasn't even a question. It was a statement. 'That is none of your damn business!' Was that how he saw her? As some vulnerable, sex-starved divorcee who need saving from herself? Regardless of her response, he was the one who had instigated the kiss, not her. And he was the one who had drawn back first, a taunting little voice reminded her.

'No, it isn't,' he agreed. His face an unreadable mask, he turned round and walked across the kitchen. 'Would you like your strawberries now?' He glanced over a broad shoulder. 'I've some ice cream in the freezer.'

Clemency's mouth almost fell open. He was suggesting that they calmly sit down and eat strawberries and ice cream? How could he look and sound as assured, as controlled as if they'd spent the last few minutes simply discussing the weather? He'd simply dismissed what had happened as being of no importance at all, a temporary, regrettable aberration. Which was all it had been, she reasoned with herself fiercely.

'Give mine to the twins,' she said curtly. She didn't know why she was so angry, felt like pummelling him with her small fists. Hurt pride because he'd been able to switch off so quickly? Because he'd been honest enough to admit that all he felt for her was a passing physical attraction—when she'd supposed he at least liked her a little? She dismissed both thoughts roughly.

'What do you want me to do?' he said quietly, his eyes moving over her rigid face. 'Apologise for kissing you?'

'Don't be so ridiculous.'

'Or apologise for not taking you to bed?'

Clemency froze as she met the taunting blue eyes, bewilderment overriding the initial spurt of anger, the cheap jibe so totally out of character from what little she knew of this man. Why was he trying to provoke her? Make her actively dislike him?

'I don't want a casual, meaningless affair with you, and I certainly don't want anything more, if that's what you're so terrified of,' she said steadily, her eyes never wavering from his. 'But I had hoped we might be friends. I was wrong,' she concluded simply, and started to walk towards the door.

'Clemency?'

She paused and turned round slowly.

'You might need this.'

She looked at him incredulously as, retrieving the tube of cream from the floor, he tossed it idly across the room. Was that supposed to be a peace offering? Catching it instinctively, she immediately hurled it back at him.

'I don't want that—or anything else from you.'

Inwardly cursing the childish outburst that had somewhat marred her dignified exit, she hurried out of the door and down the path, slamming the side gate resoundly behind her.

The telephone on the hall table started ringing the moment she stepped inside her own front door. For a moment she was tempted to ignore it and then, taking a deep breath, she picked up the receiver.

'Hello?' she enquired coolly.

'Clem?'

'Oh, it's you, David.' She instantly recognised the cheerful voice at the other end of the line.

'Do I detect a note of disappointment?' he teased. 'Who were you expecting?'

'No one,' Clemency said dismissively. Certainly not anyone of any importance.

'I'm visiting my parents in Dorchester this week and wondered if you were free for lunch one day.'

'How about Thursday?' she suggested, adding as she heard his enthusiastic acceptance, 'Thanks for your postcard, by the way. Did you have a good holiday?'

'I'll give you a minute-by-minute account illustrated with numerous snaps when I see you,' he assured her. 'Sordid details no extra charge.'

'Can't wait.' Clemency's grin widened as she replaced the phone. David Mason was a good friend, she mused affectionately, never failed to come and see her whenever he was in the area.

Her spirits rising, she made her way upstairs to her bedroom to fetch a cotton jumper, her eyes drawn instinctively to the window overlooking the neighbouring garden. She hesitated and, berating herself for her weakness, walked across to it and glanced out.

Sitting on a stool within earshot of the house, Joshua was absently eating a bowl of strawberries as he studied a newspaper balanced on his knee. A solitary but not a lonely figure. He looked self-sufficient, completely at ease with his own company. It was impossible to believe that she'd been in his arms such a short time ago.

She spun away from the window. Don't even think about it, she ordered herself. Forget the whole incident and forget Joshua Harrington, just as he had her.

That was easier said than done, Clemency discovered the following day. Smoothing sun cream onto her legs, she lay back on her lounger and sighed under her breath as she flipped through the Tuesday newspaper. Was he going to spend the whole day working on the fencing? She tossed the paper to one side and picked up a paperback book. He'd started just after nine o'clock, shortly after he'd returned from taking his sons to school.

She didn't know which was worse—the thud of the hammer as he installed the posts, the buzz of the saw as he cleared the undergrowth in his way, or the incessant, cheerful whistling that accompanied the tasks. So much for her plan to spend a lazy morning in the garden reading one of the novels she never seemed to have time for when she was working. So much for the peace and quiet of the country.

Resignedly, she slammed her book shut and rose to her feet. If you can't beat them, join them, and the grass was well overdue a cut, she admitted. She headed into the house, emerging a few minutes later clad in an old pair of denim cut-offs and a baggy green T-shirt, the key of the shed in her hand. Unlocking the door, she wheeled out the motor-mower with which she had a long-standing feud.

Checking it for oil and petrol, she murmured a silent prayer and tugged at the cord. Nothing. She tried again. A slight whirring. Another hefty tug that nearly pulled her arm from its socket. A mocking splutter. 'That's it,' she threatened. 'A car-boot sale. The scrap heap.' She kicked it with her trainer.

'You've probably flooded the engine,' a deep male voice advised helpfully. 'I should leave it for a few moments.'

Clemency whirled round. Joshua, a saw in one hand, was sauntering across the grass towards her, his faded denim shirt fastened low on his chest, gaping over his hard, tanned torso as he moved.

'Hello,' she greeted him coolly, more than a little grateful for the large sunglasses that shielded her eyes.

'Mind if I cut back the laurel at the bottom?' he enquired casually.

The unattended shrub in question was encroaching well over the boundary, Clemency admitted, but that fact didn't give him carte blanche just to wander into her back garden. It was beginning to become a habit.

'Oh, for heaven's sake, take those damn glasses off!'

'What?' she exclaimed inelegantly.

'When I grovel I prefer to do it face to face.'

The corners of Clemency's mouth tugged into an un-willing smile; the thought of this man grovelling to any-one was so utterly ludicrous.

'I'm sorry for what I said yesterday,' he said quietly and without preamble. 'It was damn puerile.'

'So why did you say it?'

'I don't know.' His mouth twisted ruefully. 'I was angry, I suppose.'

'With me?' Clemency frowned.

'With myself.' A muscle flickered along his hard jaw line. 'I hadn't intended...'

'To kiss me?' she finished helpfully. It had been far more than a mere kiss and they both knew it. 'You thought I would read more into it than was intended? Would think it signalled the start of a long, beautiful relationship?' she said dryly, her eyes meeting his squarely.

'Something like that,' he admitted.

Clemency surveyed him thoughtfully. 'Your mother was right. You are arrogant.' It was an unconscious male arrogance, rising out of his complete self-assurance.

'Possibly,' he conceded, his mouth twitching.

Clemency smiled back. His arrogance was tempered by his sense of humour, his ability to laugh at himself.

'I like you, Clemency,' he said quietly. 'I enjoy your company, but it'll never be anything more than that.'

'I know,' she said evenly, her eyes locking with his. He was tacitly offering his friendship but oddly, instead of reassuring her, the thought set off tiny warning bells in her head.

'Friends?' He quirked a dark eyebrow.

'Only if you can start my mower,' she answered with a swift grin.

Wordlessly, he placed the saw carefully on the ground and bent over the mower, the denim shirt tautening across his powerful shoulders as he pulled the cord, the engine immediately firing into life.

'Thanks,' Clemency mouthed above the noise, her stomach dipping as she met the brilliant blue gaze. Would she ever be able to regard this man in the same way as she did David Mason? Would longer acquaintance, familiarity, inure her to his physical attraction or at least enable her to view it objectively?

Taking hold of the handles of the mower, she set off across the lawn, her eyes following Joshua as he walked down to the bottom of the garden and started sawing back the laurel. That he had chosen to erect the fence himself rather than employ someone made her suspect that his powerful, lean physique owed more to a love of working outdoors than the rigours of a gym.

Getting hotter and stickier by the minute as she trailed up and down the grass, Clemency toyed with the idea of approaching the local riding stables with the offer of free grazing once a week to a suitable candidate—one of those tiny Shetland ponies might be appropriate. Enough was enough. Coming to an abrupt halt, she switched off the mower and, absently wiping her damp palms over her T-shirt, watched Joshua as he tossed the sawn-off laurel branches through the gap he'd created into his own garden.

Straightening up, he raised a dark eyebrow. 'Finished?' Pointedly his gaze encompassed the uncut grass still remaining at the bottom of the garden.

'Decided it would be more environmentally friendly

to leave it wild,' she said virtuously. Tiny beads of perspiration trickled down his neck and without warning an image of her mouth pressed into the smooth hollow at the base of his throat exploded in her head. She could almost taste the warm saltiness of his skin.

'Not to mention labour saving?' Joshua enquired innocently.

'There is of course that advantage,' Clemency agreed as if the thought had only just occurred to her, hoping fervently that he would attribute the colour in her cheeks to her physical exertion.

His mouth twitching, Joshua flicked a glance at the watch on his tanned wrist. 'Lunch-time,' he pronounced. 'Fancy walking down to the Old Oaks for a ploughman's?' he enquired idly. 'I could murder a pint.' Picking up his saw, he stepped briskly through the gap into his garden. 'Fifteen minutes suit you?' He flicked her a quick glance over his shoulder.

Clemency nodded in confirmation, hiding her swift involuntary grin as she wheeled the mower back towards the shed. Humming under her breath, she locked the shed and sped into the house. The thought of an ice-cold glass of shandy was more than a little enticing and the old-fashioned village pub he'd referred to had a reputation for simple but excellent home-made food.

A reputation it well deserved, she decided some time later, as, sitting in the shade of the huge oak tree from which the name of the inn originated, she bit into a freshly baked roll still warm from the oven.

'If that tastes as good as it smells...' Joshua murmured, picking up his knife, having slaked his immediate thirst with a long, cold swallow from his glass.

'It does,' Clemency assured him with a smile, brushing crumbs from her blue cotton skirt. With slight amusement her eyes alighted on the tickets he'd tossed casually onto the table when he'd returned from the bar with their drinks. So he'd succumbed too. It was almost impossible to live in the village and avoid buying a ticket for the forthcoming supper dance. They were on sale everywhere. She wondered if he had any real intention of attending the annual charity event or whether he'd simply purchased the tickets, as she herself had done in the village shop last week, to show willing and support the local good causes.

Idly her gaze wandered around the crowded tables surrounding them, the pub busy with its lunch-time trade, a mixture of tourists and office workers, the latter, attracted by the sunshine, having made the short drive from the nearby town. Wryly she noted the number of surreptitious female glances being directed at her companion and wondered if he was aware of them. He certainly gave no indication of it, and, perversely, that air of indifference only served to intensify his appeal, she mused, her eyes moving over the assured, strong face.

His hair, still damp from the shower when they'd set out, was now almost dry, springing up from his head in a way that made her long to slide her fingers through the thick, dark waves.

Composedly she took a sip from her glass. Resigning herself to his attraction rather than attempting to fight it somehow made it easier to deal with. It no longer caught her off-guard. And knowing that there would be no repeat of last night, that the boundaries of their relationship had been clearly defined, was like having a safety net. She could enjoy his company with impunity, she thought with a surge of confidence.

And he was good company, she admitted, his conversation light and entertaining, his dry humour exactly coinciding with her own. She discovered too that their tastes in books, music and films were similar but not so identical as to preclude discussion.

'Actually,' Joshua concluded with a grin after an animated, amicable argument about the merits of a long-running West End play, 'I haven't even seen the damn play.'

'Nor have I,' confessed Clemency with a gurgle of laughter. Swallowing her last piece of bread and cheese, she sat back contentedly in her chair, watching the antics of three kittens as they launched repeated attacks on their long-suffering mother who was sprawled out in the sun a few feet from their table. Tommy would adore them, she reflected.

'Wonder if they've managed to find homes for them yet?' Joshua murmured thoughtfully.

Having evidently overheard his remark, a pleasant-faced, middle-aged woman, a tray of empty glasses in her hand, paused by the table. 'We're still looking for a home for the little black one if you're interested,' she smiled. 'Actually the mother needs a home too,' she added, but without much hope in her voice. 'She's a stray, turned up a few days before the kittens were born.' Collecting up their empty plates, she moved on to the next table.

'Tommy?' Clemency grinned across at Joshua.

'It's more than just a phase with him,' he conceded, draining his glass. 'And I'd more or less decided to get a cat this summer now we've moved out of London and the boys are a little more responsible.' Absently picking up a pen that had been left on the table he began to doodle on a serviette. 'And having an obliging neighbour to feed it when we're away would be a decided advantage.' He looked up with a grin.

'Always supposing your obliging neighbour is in residence herself at the time,' Clemency observed dryly, and saw him raise an enquiring eyebrow.

'I've an interview in London tomorrow for a new post,' she explained casually. 'If I'm lucky enough to get it, it's going to involve a lot of travel overseas. About three weeks a month.'

'Which presumably is one of the chief attractions of the job for you?'

'Yes,' she agreed lightly, and burst into laughter as he slid the serviette across to her. A girl, a gentle caricature of herself, was looking down ferociously at a lawnmower, the latter endowed with huge, beseeching eyes beneath a sweep of very feminine, long, fluttery lashes.

'I'll be kinder to her in future,' she promised with a grin. A Josh original.

'So what will you do if you are successful?' Joshua enquired idly, resuming their previous conversation as if there had been no break in it. 'Put your cottage on the market?'

She frowned. 'I hadn't thought of doing so.'

'It would be more practical to have a flat in town if you're going to be away most of the time,' he drawled.

'I suppose so,' she conceded. It was as if he was actively encouraging her to move away. Any moment now, he'd be offering to erect the 'for sale' sign.

'Much easier to maintain than a house and garden,' he continued carelessly. 'After all, you wouldn't really need much more than a base in England.'

A base, not a home. Her eyes jerked to his. 'I'm not

your ex-wife.' Oh, God, she couldn't believe she'd just said that.

'And what the hell is that supposed to mean?'

Silently, she finished off her drink.

'Clemency?' Joshua prompted quietly.

'I'm sorry, all right?' She raised her hands in front of her. 'Could you just let it drop, please?' How could she explain what she'd meant when she didn't even know herself? Didn't know why his remark had caught her so much on the raw?

He shrugged and glanced at his watch. 'Shall we make a move? I'd like to finish the fencing before the boys get back from school.' He rose to his feet.

'Yes, of course,' Clemency returned, echoing the cool courtesy in his voice.

She started to follow him across the grass and then paused, swiftly picking up the serviette he'd given her and slipping it into her shoulder bag.

The short walk back to her cottage seemed endless, Joshua finally breaking the silence when they reached her front gate.

'Good luck tomorrow. I hope you get the job.' He paused almost imperceptibly. 'If that's what you want.'

'Thank you,' she returned politely. Of course that was what she wanted. She started briskly up the path and faltered. Wasn't it? Come on, she chided herself abruptly. Why else would she have applied for the position, for heaven's sake?

CHAPTER FIVE

JUST as Clemency had feared. The man who operated
the sole village taxi was already out on a call and would
be at least twenty minutes. Summoning a taxi from further afield would take even longer. Trying to quell her
mounting frustration, Clemency replaced the telephone
receiver. She was going to miss her train and she had
no one to blame but herself. She'd accepted that she
might lose the job to a more qualified candidate, but to
lose it through her own stupidity!

There was one other option. Hesitating only for a second, she picked up the jacket of her coral suit and her
matching leather handbag and sped out of the house,
down her drive and up the adjacent one. Of course, he
might not even be in, might not have returned straight
home after walking the twins to school.

She couldn't disguise her relief as the door swung
open almost immediately after she'd pressed the bell.

'Hello, Clemency,' Joshua greeted her easily, and
frowned. 'What's up?'

Was her agitation that obvious? 'My car won't start,'
she started in a rush. 'And...'

'What time's your train?' he intervened crisply.

'Nine-thirty-five.'

'Right. I'll fetch my keys.'

Before she could thank him, he was halfway down the
hall, returning a few seconds later with the car keys in
his hand.

If the roles had been reversed, would she have acted quite so decisively and swiftly? Clemency wondered as he unlocked the passenger door of the sleek silver saloon. He'd summed up the situation immediately, hadn't hesitated or wasted time with superfluous questions.

Her eyes flicked over his strong, assured profile as he folded his long, lean frame into the seat beside her, knowing that she hadn't really doubted for a second that he would come to her assistance.

As the powerful car glided smoothly into the lane she saw Joshua's quick, speculative glance at the stationary vehicle in her drive and pre-empted the inevitable query. Might as well come clean, she thought with an inward sigh.

'I've run out of petrol.' Or would certainly have done so had she attempted to reach the nearest garage, some six miles outside the village.

She wasn't surprised to see the dark eyebrows shoot up, hadn't been able to believe it herself when she'd seen her fuel gauge this morning. She'd intended to fill up the tank on Monday, on her way to the coast. That she'd forgotten to do so, hadn't even noticed how perilously close her gauge was to empty on the return trip, was completely uncharacteristic and incomprehensible.

'I'll pick up a can of petrol on my way back from the station,' Joshua said casually.

'Thanks.' Clemency looked at him thoughtfully. Was that all he was going to say on the matter? No little crack about women drivers?

She sat back comfortably in her seat, looking out of the window at the passing fields, her sense of urgency evaporating. If she missed her train, she missed it. It was hardly a matter of life or death, she thought philosophically.

'Do you miss London?' Joshua asked idly as he manoeuvred the car carefully and skilfully through a herd of cows plodding slowly back towards their field after milking.

'I thought I would,' she said reflectively. 'But, no, I don't.' She looked up at the cloudless azure sky. 'Especially not on a glorious day like this,' she added wistfully.

'A day for meandering over the Purbeck Hills, not fighting your way through congested city streets, hmm?' he murmured, his eyes never straying from the road as he joined the busy dual carriageway.

'Mmm,' she agreed, shaken by the image his innocent words had conjured up in her head. She and Joshua, sauntering over the Studland cliffs, hand in hand... For Pete's sake, how adolescent could she get?

'Or horse riding in the New Forest,' she said determinedly, and saw Joshua's raised eyebrow.

'I thought...?'

'I rather like the idea of ambling along on my trusty steed in theory. It's just the practice I shy away from,' she explained with a swift grin, gathering up her jacket and handbag as Joshua turned into the station yard.

She would catch the train with five minutes to spare. 'Thanks,' she said gratefully, reaching for the handle as he drew to a halt in front of the entrance.

'Which train are you planning to catch back?'

She planned to spend the afternoon with her mother and catch a train back in the early evening, to avoid the worst of the rush hour. 'The eighteen-forty from Waterloo,' she told him as she scrambled out. 'But I'll catch a taxi,' she called back firmly over a slim shoulder as she sped into the station and frowned. In which case it had been a little unnecessary to be quite so specific about her train time, hadn't it?

'Let me know the minute you hear about the job, darling, and come down for a weekend soon.'

'I will,' Clemency promised, smiling affectionately at her mother. Each armed with a carrier bag, the result of their afternoon shopping expedition, they walked along the platform towards the rear of the stationary train and stopped by a half-empty carriage.

'Your father and I do worry about you living on your own.'

'I'm twenty-seven,' Clemency said gently.

'Miles from anywhere.'

'It's a fifteen-minute walk to the village.'

'It wouldn't be so bad if someone moved in next door.'

'They have actually,' Clemency murmured casually.

'The Anderson house has been sold at last? Oh, I am so pleased. Your father and I hated the idea of you living next to an empty house.'

Clemency hid her grin, exasperation with her mother as always tempered by love.

'So what are they like?'

'Very pleasant. Two small boys,' Clemency said firmly.

'A family.' Her mother smiled happily. 'Take care, darling.'

'You too, Mum. Give my love to Dad.'

Giving her mother a hug, Clemency boarded the train, wondering a little guiltily why she'd been deliberately ambiguous about her new neighbour, why she'd been so reluctant to mention Joshua. Her lips curved as she sat down by the window, placing her carrier bag on the empty seat beside her. 'Pleasant' wasn't exactly the bland, innocuous adjective that came uppermost to mind when she thought about Joshua Harrington—and thinking about him was fast becoming one of her most popular pastimes, she acknowledged uneasily.

She leant back in her seat and closed her eyes, suddenly hoping fervently that her interview had been successful.

She saw the tall, commanding figure the moment the train slid into the station. Standing near the ticket barrier, he was dressed in tailored black trousers, a crisp white shirt with a blue silk tie knotted at his throat and a discreetly checked dark jacket that fitted the width of his shoulders to perfection. He looked devastating.

Catching her breath sharply, Clemency stepped off the train, the lazy smile of welcome on Joshua's face as he strode towards her making her weak.

'Taxi, ma'am?' he drawled as he reached her.

She couldn't think of a flip rejoinder, felt as gauche as a teenager, completely overwhelmed by him. 'Where are the twins?' she asked lightly instead.

'They're staying with my parents overnight,' he explained casually, shortening his strides to match hers as they made their way to the exit. 'Mum and Dad are flying out to Canada tomorrow and won't see the boys for a couple of weeks.' He grinned. 'And my mother is doubtlessly spoiling them abysmally tonight to make up for it.'

Clemency grinned back, fascinated as always at the

way his eyes seemed to change shade, become an even more dazzling blue, when he laughed. Oh, no. She'd left her carrier bag on the train, the tail lights of which were fast disappearing down the line.

'So how did the interview go?' Joshua murmured as they reached the car park.

'Not bad,' she said noncommittally. She'd telephone the lost-property office first thing in the morning, she decided. At least the bag had only contained a couple of T-shirts she'd spotted in a sale; the hideously expensive jacket she'd fallen in love with and been egged on by her mother to buy had fortunately required minor alterations and would be sent to her direct.

'Quietly confident?' His eyes teased her as he unlocked the passenger door of the silver saloon and held it open for her.

She smiled as she slid into her seat. She was certainly more confident about her career prospects than she was in her ability to deal with this man.

'Thanks for meeting me,' she said with a casualness she was far from feeling.

'I confess I had an ulterior motive in doing so,' he said solemnly. 'Have you eaten yet? And do you like Chinese food?' He grinned. 'The correct answer to the first question is a negative, and to the second a very enthusiastic affirmative.'

With a great deal of effort Clemency kept her face straight. 'No, I haven't eaten,' she said obediently. She took a deep breath. 'And I adore Chinese food,' she gushed.

'Good,' Joshua said with satisfaction, his eyes laughing into hers. 'Because I hate eating alone, and Chinese food is most definitely for sharing.'

Sharing with friends, Clemency amended silently and determinedly.

'No cheating,' Joshua admonished with mock severity as Clemency stealthily picked up a fork.

Grinning at him across the white damask-covered table, she returned to her chopsticks, her proficiency with them far inferior to his.

'Sharing, hmm?' she teased him. 'You're managing to eat twice as much as I am.'

Neither of them familiar with Chinese restaurants in the area, they had selected one at random up a side street in Bournemouth, their choice proving to be a fortuitous one, the food and service both excellent.

'I may have a slight advantage,' Joshua conceded with a swift answering grin. 'Laura and I took a couple of years off after we left university and spent about six months in Hong Kong teaching English.'

There was no change of inflection in his voice when he mentioned his ex-wife, Clemency mused, his expression giving her no clue as to the memories that must be unfolding in his head.

'What else did you do?' she asked, fascinated by the voluntary insight into his past, a past which had very much included the woman he'd once loved.

He shrugged casually. 'The usual. Back-packed our way around Europe, across Australia.'

Something she'd once dreamed of doing with Simon, she reflected a little wistfully, but he'd never been enthusiastic about the idea.

Unobserved, her gaze wandered over Joshua's face, the rugged male features softened by the subtle lighting, his eyes beneath the thick black lashes darkened to navy blue. Maybe it was the effects of the wine or maybe it was the serene ambience of the restaurant, but it was the first time she'd felt so completely at ease in his company, their conversation light, good-humoured and undemanding, the occasional silences, like now, unconstrained.

With a small sigh of contentment she placed her chopsticks on her empty plate and leant back in her chair, enveloped in a rosy glow of utter well-being.

'Coffee?' Joshua suggested as the waiter quietly and efficiently cleared the table.

'Yes, please,' she murmured lazily, her eyes drifting around the restaurant. Half-empty when they'd arrived, she was startled to see that most tables were now occupied. She murmured her thanks as the waiter placed a coffee cup in front of her. How long had that couple been sitting at the table behind Joshua? she wondered as she took a sip of coffee, surprised that she hadn't even noticed their arrival.

'People watching?' Joshua raised a quizzical eyebrow, smiling at her.

She smiled back as she surveyed him over the rim of her cup, suspecting that, given his profession, he was equally fascinated by his fellow man. But he never made judgements on them, she reflected, thinking about his cartoons, his humour never cruel.

'I suppose we'd better make a move,' Joshua murmured after they'd both declined more coffee.

'Suppose so,' she agreed soporifically, almost too comfortable to move.

'What you need is a brisk walk by the sea,' Joshua informed her vigorously as he signalled for the bill.

'Masochist,' she groaned, and then grinned. 'Make it

a gentle stroll and you're on.' Handbag and jacket, she reminded herself firmly as she stood up.

As they stepped out into the warm night air, they both stood for a moment, gazing up at the velvety sky.

'No stars,' Clemency murmured a little sadly.

'Too many lights to see them.' Reaching casually for her hand, Joshua tucked it companionably through the crook of his arm.

Warm happiness stealing through her, Clemency sauntered by his side as he led the way down the hill to the sea. The tide was in and they walked along by the sea wall, listening to the gentle lapping of the waves below.

'The Isle of Wight,' Joshua murmured softly as they came to a halt, pointing out the distant lights across the expanse of dark water.

Lost in a warm bubble of unreality, Clemency smiled in the darkness, blissfully aware of Joshua's arm resting lightly on her shoulder as he stood just behind her. She turned her head slightly, her eyes on a level with the square jaw, her sense of smell teased by the evocative scent of expensive masculine aftershave. Slowly her gaze moved upwards, settled on the decisive mouth. It would be so easy just to reach up those few short, tantalising inches, she thought dreamily.

She felt his hand on her shoulder tighten and tilted her face up, adrenalin shivering through her as his eyes locked with hers, the anticipation almost unbearable.

'It's getting late.' His voice gruff, Joshua's hand dropped from her shoulder.

Unable to trust her voice, Clemency nodded silently, keeping her face averted as they began retracing their steps. He made no attempt to take her arm, the studied gap between them as uncomfortable to Clemency as the silence. The mood of easy companionship between them had evaporated completely. She suddenly felt cold, empty and inexplicably lonely, mentally isolated from the tall figure beside her.

Even if he had kissed her—and he'd found it remarkably easy to resist the fleeting temptation to do so—it would have meant nothing, a few moments of sensuous pleasure that he would have probably forgotten by the time they reached the car.

And would it have been any different for her? A tiny chill ran down her stiffening spine. What exactly did she want from this man?

'Nothing. Nothing at all!' Clemency disclaimed firmly out loud as she woke up on Thursday morning. Arms folded behind her head, she gazed up at the rays of sunlight dancing on her bedroom ceiling and grinned. That old adage about things looking different in the morning was certainly true. She couldn't understand what she'd been in such a tizz about last night or why she'd been so convinced when Joshua had dropped her off that the evening had been a total disaster. Simply because he hadn't kept up a flow of inane chatter on the drive home. She hadn't exactly been garrulous herself!

As the telephone on her bedside table rang she idly stretched out a hand to pick up the receiver. Probably her mother, the only person who would call her at this hour of the morning. Absently her eyes dropped to her alarm clock, widening with disbelief as she registered the hour. Half past nine?

Reeling off her number, she tugged the duvet up around her, exposing her slender feet.

'Busy?' enquired just about the last voice she'd expected to hear, the laconic question throwing her even more off-balance.

'Not specially,' she said vaguely, noting with an almost objective curiosity the way her toes were suddenly curling into the mattress.

'Right, I'll pick you up in half an hour,' Joshua announced briskly. 'Jeans and sensible shoes.' The line went dead.

Well, really! Momentarily infuriated by his high-handedness, Clemency replaced the receiver and then slowly she began to grin. Throwing back the duvet, she leapt out of bed, knowing that she could no more resist the imperious summons than fly to the moon. A summons that just proved how groundless her fears about last night had been.

Jeans and sensible shoes, hmm? She had an awful suspicion that she knew exactly what was in store for her.

The suspicion was confirmed some thirty minutes later when she opened her front door to find Joshua standing there, a hard hat in his hand. Although, she didn't notice the hat immediately, Joshua for once completely upstaged by the two horses tethered to the gate post behind him.

'Your trusty steed,' he smiled blandly.

Censuring the reply that immediately formed in her head, she gave a careless smile, nonchalantly taking hold of the proffered hat. Her eyes darted back to the gate post. Couldn't he at least have found a smaller model? The petite version? Come to think of it, where exactly had they come from?

'Holly Farm,' he explained in answer to her question as they walked down the drive.

Having a slight acquaintance with the owner of the local riding school to which he'd referred, Clemency was surprised that Joshua had been permitted to hire the horses without supervision. Though he certainly seemed to know what he was doing, she reflected as he released one of the horses and started adjusting the stirrup leathers.

The airy smile beginning to make her face ache, she approached the grey mare cautiously and tentatively patted its neck. Why on earth was she letting Joshua put her through this ordeal?

'Ready?' Joshua asked casually.

She hesitated, her eyes moving from the horse to the still, lean figure, and then inexplicably her nerves vanished, her trust in him absolute.

She nodded, concentrating on his instructions as he positioned the stirrup for her left foot.

'Okay, up you jump. That's it. Slip your other foot into the stirrup. Well done.'

Clutching both the reins and the pommel of the saddle, Clemency grinned down at him, flushed with success.

'So far, so good?' he laughed softly at the delight on her face.

'So far, so good.' Feeling quite ridiculously happy, she watched as Joshua attached a leading rein to the mare's bridle, and then without the aid of stirrups vaulted lightly into his own saddle.

'Wondered if I could still do that,' he murmured with satisfaction. He gathered up his reins and led off at a steady walk down the lane, keeping Clemency close to his side. 'One of my uncles owns a dude ranch in America, and Laura and I used to spend working holidays over there when we were students. He used to be a stunt rider...'

'And taught you a few tricks of the trade?' Clemency smiled. Did the ease with which he referred to Laura mean some of the scars were beginning to heal? That it no longer hurt him to think back to the carefree days when they'd obviously been happy together? Or did it simply indicate that she was still constantly in his thoughts?

'Try and let go of the saddle.' His lips twitched slightly as he looked down at her.

Tentatively, she obeyed him.

'That's it. Grip with your legs and shorten your reins a little. Good.'

'Think I'm a natural?' She grinned with renewed confidence, glowing under his praise, and with a rush of bravado lifted a hand to wave nonchalantly at the two small children who had rushed to their front gate at the sound of horses' hooves. That was a decided mistake, she conceded as she lost both her balance and her reins and ended up in an undignified sprawl halfway down the mare's neck, clutching at its name.

'Maybe just a tad less confidence?' Joshua suggested as she righted herself.

She grinned to herself as he turned off the lane onto a bridle path through a canopy of trees. He was evidently innocent of the fact that it was he who inspired that confidence. Made her feel that she was capable of doing anything she set her mind to. It was a glorious sensation.

'Look over to your left,' Joshua said softly, reining his horse to a halt.

Her eyes immediately followed his gaze, and glowed with delight at the sight of the small herd of fallow deer grazing in the clearing, oblivious to their silent watchers. Instinctively her gaze flicked back to Joshua, wanting to share her pleasure with him. He was sitting erect in the saddle, eyes narrowed against the sun, the chestnut mare beneath him alert, ears pricked forwards. They were both completely motionless, could have been sculptured out of bronze, the sheer, vital beauty of man and horse making Clemency's throat constrict, the deer forgotten.

'We'll start to head back now,' Joshua decided as they moved off slowly, branching off down a side track which Clemency knew from her own explorations would come out at the top of the lane near Holly Farm. 'You're going to be stiff enough as it is tomorrow,' he warned as she gave him a look of disappointment. 'Especially,' he added with a swift grin, 'after you've tried trotting.'

Even if she was too stiff to crawl out of bed tomorrow, she wouldn't care. It would have been worth it. Feeling as exhilarated as if she'd just climbed Mount Everest, Clemency determinedly placed one candyfloss leg in front of another as she walked down the lane by Joshua's side.

'I must settle up with you for the hire of the horses.' Sun glinting on her tousled red-gold curls, she looked up at him happily. 'And for last night,' she added, remembering with a flicker of guilt that she had omitted to pay for her share of the Chinese meal.

'Your shout next time,' he said easily, his teeth very white as he smiled down at her.

She smiled back without protest, the words sending an immediate tingle of warmth through her. So there was going to be a next time. As they reached her front gate, she dug her hand into the pocket of her jeans and groaned inwardly.

'I, um, seem to have forgotten my key,' she muttered, and for some reason the look of tolerant amusement in the blue eyes irked her even more than her own carelessness.

Walking up the front path, he surveyed the cottage, his gaze alighting thoughtfully on the open bathroom window.

'I should be able to reach that with a ladder.'

'Thanks.' It was the second time in as many days he'd come to her rescue.

'I simply don't do things like this,' she suddenly exploded. 'I've never locked myself out of the house before. I've never run out of petrol before.' And she'd never left anything behind her on a train before. Before...before Joshua Harrington had sauntered back into her life. Oh, God.

'Temper tantrum over.' She forced the light smile to her lips.

There was no answering smile on the straight mouth, no trace of lingering amusement in his eyes, the blue shadowed depths unreadable as they flicked over her face. He might be perceptive but he wasn't a mind reader, Clemency reassured herself firmly.

She glanced automatically over her shoulder as she heard the sound of a car drawing up on the verge, a feeling of utter resignation sweeping over her as she immediately recognised the russet-haired man who bounded out of the driver's seat. Forgetting she'd arranged to have lunch with David today was pretty much par for the course right now, wasn't it?

'It appears that you have a visitor,' Joshua drawled.

'Yes,' Clemency said brightly, moving down the path to meet David.

'Clemmy.' He greeted her with a huge bear hug and a resounding kiss on the cheek, and then grinned affably at Joshua. It was the way he'd always greeted her, it was the way he greeted his sisters, his mother, his aunts, and yet today, acutely conscious of their observer, it made Clemency feel uncharacteristically awkward.

'Joshua, this is a friend of mine, David Mason.' She wished David would remove his arm from her shoulder. 'David, Joshua Harrington. My neighbour,' she added casually, and saw the dark eyebrows rise slightly. She refused to meet his eyes. Whatever Joshua Harrington was to her—and that was something she refused to even think about right now—he wasn't merely a neighbour.

'David.' Smiling easily, Joshua held out a lean hand towards the shorter, slighter man. It wasn't until David's arm slipped from her shoulder that Clemency realised Joshua had, presumably quite deliberately, extended his left hand. Her eyes shot to his face, but the bland smile remained intact.

'I'll go and fetch the ladder,' he drawled.

'I've very stupidly locked myself out,' Clemency explained lightly to David.

'Problem solved,' David said cheerfully, and, fishing in the pocket of his jacket, produced a key attached to a leather tag with the letters 'CA' emblazoned in gold.

Clemency blinked. What on earth was David doing with the spare key to her home? The same question had evidently occurred to Joshua, she realised, registering the speculation in the blue eyes as they rested on the other man. Oh, let him draw his own conclusions about her relationship with David. And, if they were the wrong ones, so be it. She didn't owe him any explanations.

'Nice to meet you, David.' The blue eyes settled briefly on Clemency, their expression giving nothing away. 'Be seeing you.'

She nodded, wondering why she had the most awful urge to run after him as he strode down the path.

'Pretty impressive chap, your *neighbour*.'

Conscious that she'd completely forgotten his presence for a few seconds, Clemency turned towards David, controlling her immediate irritation at the innuendo in his teasing voice.

She shrugged, not answering.

'Is he married?' he enquired, following her into the hall as she opened the door.

'Divorced,' she said lightly, and grinned. 'David Mason, you're worse than my mother!'

He grinned back, unoffended, and then wrinkled his nose slightly. 'Clemmy, love of my life…'

'I smell of horse,' Clemency finished for him as she led him through the kitchen and out onto the small patio. 'I've been riding this morning,' she said casually, and saw the disbelief in his face as he sat down on a chair.

'You've what? But you…' David paused, his eyes glinting. 'With your neighbour?' As he saw the confirmation on her face he let out a little whoop. 'Well, if he managed to persuade you onto a horse, it must be love!'

'Don't be so damn ridiculous!' Clemency flared, and saw the surprise on his face.

'I was only joking,' he said mildly.

'Yes, I know.' She'd been equally surprised by her overreaction. 'I'm sorry,' she said quietly, recovering herself quickly. 'Now, amuse yourself for five minutes while I have a quick shower,' she ordered him with a grin, handing him a newspaper. 'Fancy going to the Old Oaks for lunch?'

'Is that the thatched pub near the green? The one with the stunning brunette behind the bar?'

'David Mason, it's about time you grew up!' she admonished him affectionately.

'That's a conclusion I've more or less reached myself just lately,' he said quietly.

Clemency frowned. His face for once was completely serious. 'David?' she prompted.

'Tell you later.' He smiled.

Armed with a glass of lemonade and a menu, Clemency threaded her way through the crowded lounge bar to a recently vacated table by an open window. It was too hot to sit out today. Even the grey and white cat had sought the shade of the shrubbery, she noted, glancing out of the window. Only one kitten today, she registered, the little black one, the other two presumably having now gone to their new homes.

Taking a grateful sip from her cold glass, her eyes moved over David's pleasant, open face as he sat down opposite her, but for a second seeing an entirely different set of features in her mind.

'Where did you get my spare door key from?' she suddenly asked, memory jogged.

'Ian asked me to give it back to you. He took it home with him by mistake the last time he came down for the weekend.'

'Typical of my brother.' Clemency smiled. Mystery solved.

'Joshua didn't look over-impressed with my conjuring

trick.' David paused and grinned. 'Or with my appearance full stop.'

'What would you like to eat? My treat.' Calmly Clemency handed him the menu. He was only teasing her, the way he'd been teasing her for years, and she wasn't going to bite. Especially when the subject of her baiting had just walked through the door.

For a moment Joshua paused in the doorway, as if adjusting his eyes to the gloom after the glaring sunlight outside, and then moved purposefully towards the bar, his height and breadth creating an immediate path through the crowd.

He hadn't seen them, seemed oblivious to the number of female eyes, hers included, following his progress across the room. Swiftly Clemency took another sip from her glass, conscious that, for some totally illogical reason, she was actually relieved that Joshua hadn't noticed her sitting here with David.

'Home-made steak and kidney pudding,' David announced, putting the menu down.

'In this weather?' She looked at him disbelievingly. 'I think I'll just have a sandwich.' She'd been ravenous after her riding lesson but her appetite seemed to have deserted her. Picking up her handbag, she edged her way through the throng to place their food order and came to an abrupt halt.

Joshua was standing at the bar right in front of her, nursing a pint glass in his hand. Eyes slightly narrowed, he looked completely preoccupied with his own thoughts, indifferent to the activity around him.

Clemency hesitated. His shuttered expression, his air of cool aloofness, discouraged intrusion, signalled a strong desire for his own company. She was still hesitating when Joshua suddenly turned his head.

'Hello, Clemency.' His expression barely altered as he saw her, evincing neither surprise nor pleasure at her appearance, making her suddenly suspect that he had already been aware of her presence in the pub. Then, without warning, the straight mouth quirked at the corners, the slow, lazy smile working its usual magic, instantly transforming the harsh features.

But *she* wasn't the recipient of that smile. The warm blue eyes weren't focused on *her*, she realised immediately, her stomach giving an odd little dip, but the pretty dark-haired woman who'd just walked through the door and was now making her way towards them.

'Sorry I'm late, Josh.' The brunette greeted him with a light kiss on the cheek. 'Would you believe it? I forgot to bring the cat basket with me to work this morning and had to make a quick detour home to pick it up.' She turned to Clemency with a friendly smile. 'Hello.'

'Anna, this is Clemency Adams,' Joshua drawled, adding almost as an afterthought, 'A neighbour of mine.'

Now, that was really childish. For a brief second Clemency's eyes locked into the blue ones, and then swiftly, averting her gaze, she returned the other girl's smile.

So this was the mysterious Anna whose role in Joshua's life she wasn't even going to attempt to guess, although it was presumably more than the provider of cat baskets. He'd evidently decided to get the kitten, then, she surmised, wondering why on earth it should suddenly matter to her that he hadn't mentioned his intention this morning. Why should he? Minor changes in his household were hardly any concern of hers.

'What would you like to drink, Anna?' Joshua enquired.

'Just a Coke, please.' She grinned at Clemency. 'I'm showing a prospective buyer around a bungalow at two and I don't want to breathe fumes all over them.'

'You work for an estate agent?'

As Anna nodded in confirmation, Clemency found herself wishing quite irrationally that she hadn't taken such an instant liking to the other woman. Was that how Joshua had met her? When he had been looking for a house in the area? No. The easy familiarity between the two of them was indicative of a long, not new acquaintance.

'Clemency?' Joshua raised a dark eyebrow at her.

'Not for me, thanks.' Her voice reflected his own courteous but coolly impersonal tone. 'I was just about to order some food.'

'Food!' Anna grinned up at Joshua as he handed her a glass.

'I take it that you're starving as per usual?'

Clemency glanced away, the teasing expression in the amused blue eyes gazing down at the brunette making her stomach muscles tighten. Swiftly attracting the attention of one of the bar staff, she placed her order.

'Where are you sitting?'

'Over by the window?' Automatically, she glanced over her shoulder towards David, and, aware that Joshua had followed her gaze, shot him a swift glance, wondering if she imagined the shadow of displeasure in the blue eyes as they rested briefly on the russet-haired man. Just adolescent wishful thinking? It was disturbing to know that for one shaming moment she'd actually hoped that he might find David's appearance in her life as unsettling as she did Anna in his.

As she fumbled in her handbag to retrieve her purse, a white serviette fluttered to the floor, landing by Joshua's foot. Oh, hell. Her Josh original. She scrambled to retrieve it, but Joshua was there before her.

'Thank you,' she said stiffly as he handed it to her. Too much to hope that he hadn't immediately recognised his own work. The dark blue eyes were unreadable as they locked fleetingly with hers. Tucking the serviette awkwardly back into her handbag, she turned to pay her bill, conscious of Anna's thoughtful brown eyes resting on her slightly flushed face.

'See you again soon, I hope,' she smiled as Clemency moved away from the bar.

Clemency smiled back, thinking that had circumstances been different she could have quite easily become friends with the other girl. And what circumstances were those exactly? a small voice enquired as, exchanging casual nods with Joshua, she started walking back towards her table. She ignored it.

'So what's this news you've been bursting to tell me?' Clemency enquired brightly as she slipped back into her seat, determinedly concentrating her whole attention on David.

David grinned and spread his arms theatrically. 'I'm in love.'

Clemency grinned back. So what was new? David fell in—and out of—love as often as most men changed their shirts.

'No, this time it's different,' he protested as he saw the scepticism on her face. Opening his wallet, he carefully passed her a small photo. 'Jane's different.'

The sturdy brown-haired girl clad in a scruffy pair of jeans, pulling a face at the camera, certainly bore no physical resemblance to the cool, sophisticated, leggy blondes who normally attracted his fleeting affection. Thoughtfully, Clemency's eyes moved back to David's face.

'She's special,' he said simply. 'I can't explain it but when I'm with her...I just feel so alive. As if I could do anything in the world.'

Clemency jolted, her eyes of their own volition flicking around the room. They had moved away from the bar and were sitting at a table by the door, Joshua's gaze concentrated on Anna's animated face. Clemency's chest tightened. Seeing Joshua so engrossed with another woman didn't just unsettle her, it actually *hurt* she admitted with a cold ripple of shock. That she had no earthly right to feel that way somehow made it even worse.

'I know it's trite, but I feel as if I've finally found that missing piece of jigsaw.'

Yes, it was trite. Clemency's eyes dropped to her glass. But however banal David's words, she realised with a slow, sinking feeling, she knew exactly what he meant.

'I really love her, Clemmy,' David said softly, and then added in a rush, 'The only trouble is I'm not a hundred per cent certain that she feels the same.'

Clemency's eyes shot to his face. She'd never seen him look so completely vulnerable.

'I want to marry her, Clemmy.' He tried his usual jaunty grin but it didn't work. 'But I'm terrified to ask her in case she says no.'

'Oh, David.' That look of utter despondency in his

PLAY "LUCKY 7" AND GET
THREE FREE GIFTS!

HOW TO PLAY:

1. With a coin, carefully scratch off the silver box at the right. Then check the claim chart to see what we have for you — **FREE BOOKS** and a gift — **ALL YOURS! ALL FREE!**

2. Send back this card and you'll receive brand-new Harlequin Romance® novels. These books have a cover price of $3.50 each, but they are yours to keep absolutely free.

3. There's no catch. You're under no obligation to buy anything. We charge nothing — ZERO — for your first shipmer And you don't have to make any minimum number of purchases — not even one!

4. The fact is thousands of readers enjoy receiving books by mail from the Harlequin Reader Service® months before they're available in stores. They like the convenience of home delivery and they love our discount prices!

5. We hope that after receiving your free books you'll want to remain a subscriber. But the choice is yours — to continue or cancel, any time at all! So why not take us up on o invitation, with no risk of any kind. You'll be glad you did!

YOURS FREE!

PLAY LUCKY 7 FOR THIS EXCITING FREE GIFT!

THIS SURPRISE MYSTERY GIFT COULD BE YOURS FREE WHEN YOU PLAY

LUCKY 7!

PLAY THE

LUCKY 7

SLOT MACHINE GAME!

Just scratch off the silver box with a coin. Then check below to see the gifts you get!

YES!

I have scratched off the silver box. Please send me all the gifts for which I qualify. I understand I am under no obligation to purchase any books, as explained on the back and on the opposite page.

116 HDL CGUN
(U-H-R-07/98)

Name _____
PLEASE PRINT CLEARLY

Address _____ Apt.#

City _____ State _____ Zip _____

WORTH TWO FREE BOOKS
PLUS A BONUS MYSTERY GIFT!

WORTH TWO FREE BOOKS!

WORTH ONE FREE BOOK!

TRY AGAIN!

The Harlequin Reader Service® — Here's how it works

Accepting free books places you under no obligation to buy anything. You may keep the books and gift and return the shipping statement marked "cancel." If you do not cancel, about a month later we'll send you 6 additional novels, and bill you just $2.90 each, plus 25¢ delivery per book and applicable sales tax, if any.* That's the complete price — and compared to cover prices of $3.50 each — quite a bargain! You may cancel at any time, but if you choose to continue, every month we'll send you 6 more books, which you may either purchase at the discount price...or return to us and cancel your subscription.

*Terms and prices subject to change without notice. Sales tax applicable in N.Y.

eyes was unbearable. 'She'd be crazy to say no,' she told him with fierce loyalty.

'Can I quote you on that?' Abruptly, David leant across the table and kissed her on the cheek. 'You're great, Clemmy,' he said quietly. 'I could never understand what the hell Simon saw in...' He shut his mouth abruptly, wincing.

'Lisa?' Clemency said quietly. Her eyes didn't waver from his face. 'It's all right, David, I know Simon first became involved with Lisa while we were still married.' She paused slightly. 'I take it you knew right from the start? I did sometimes wonder about that.'

David's fair skin showed his acute discomfort. 'Would you have thanked me if I'd told you at the time?' he mumbled.

'Shot the messenger?' She tried to grin but couldn't, the sense of betrayal too acute. 'All those evenings you and Simon were supposedly playing squash...'

'I told him what a fool he was.'

But he'd still let himself be used as an alibi. Clemency bit her lip and, turning her head, stared out of the window, her eyes alighting on the grey and white cat still fast asleep in the shrubbery. She gazed at it for a long while and then frowned as she registered the kitten's absence.

Her eyes moved slowly to the door. Joshua and Anna had gone too.

'I'm sorry, Clem,' David muttered unhappily.

'It doesn't matter. Not now,' she said quietly. But, her worst suspicions confirmed, she knew that nothing would ever be the same between them, that fundamental trust gone for ever. Lisa. And now David. Her two childhood friends. She'd lost them both.

'Clemmy…'

'It's all right, David,' she said swiftly, her gaze jerking to the window again as she heard the loud, protracted cry of distress. The grey and white cat had woken up, and was searching desperately for her kitten. Somehow, it seemed the last straw. Clemency felt the tears sting her eyes.

CHAPTER SIX

WHOEVER that was, she didn't feel like talking to them. Wasn't in the mood to speak to anyone this evening.

With a set face, Clemency ignored the telephone and, reaching up to the kitchen cupboard above her head, retrieved a glass bowl. What was the female equivalent of a misogynist? She extracted a fork from a drawer and slammed it shut. Oh, to hell with Simon. To hell with David. And to hell with Joshua Harrington.

The anger evaporated as suddenly as it had ignited. Simon belonged to the past, had long ceased to matter enough to hurt her. And David... Oh, poor David. He'd still looked so hangdog when he'd left this afternoon. She'd call him in a day or two, she decided.

Gingerly she moved across the tiled floor and reached into the fridge for a box of eggs. And she had no justification at all for adding Joshua's name to the roll call in the first place. He hadn't lied to her, or betrayed her. He was just responsible for the fact that she was almost too stiff to walk this evening.

Her mouth began to curve involuntarily. This morning had been fun, she mused wistfully. Her smile stiffened. It hadn't been quite so much fun seeing Joshua with Anna, though, had it?

Abruptly, she replaced the box of eggs in the fridge, the thought of an omelette suddenly as unappetising as had seemed her half-eaten sandwich at lunch-time.

'Clemency?'

She whirled round as a shadow fell over the kitchen, the evening sunshine blocked by the towering figure standing on the threshold of the open back door.

'For Pete's sake, Joshua, why can't you ever knock?' He was the last person she felt like seeing.

'I'm sorry if I startled you,' he said quietly, moving uninvited into the kitchen, 'But I assumed you were in the garden. Didn't you hear the telephone?'

She didn't answer him, registering the lines of tension etched into his face for the first time, the unmistakable anxiety in his dark eyes. 'What's the matter?' she said swiftly.

'Jamie has suspected appendicitis,' he said without preamble. 'The doctor's ordered an ambulance which should be here very soon.'

'And you'd like me to mind Tommy while you go to the hospital,' Clemency said quietly, already moving across the room to close the window and lock the back door.

'He was complaining of a stomach ache when I met him from school.' Joshua followed her down the hall and out the front door. 'I should have taken it more seriously straight away, but he seemed to forget all about it with the excitement of the kitten. Key?' he reminded her just before she turned to slam the door.

'In my pocket,' she assured him, patting her jeans, the brief smile touching his lips as he looked down at her, relieving the strain in his eyes. But only momentarily.

'He's so little,' he muttered gruffly, and for a second his guard slipped, the strong face completely stripped of its habitual assurance. Then abruptly he swung away on down the drive, Clemency doing her level best to keep up with his rapid, urgent strides.

A small pyjama-clad figure came to meet them as they walked through the front door.

'Jamie's been a little bit sick, Daddy,' Tommy announced matter-of-factly. 'But I helped the doctor look after him.'

'Good chap,' Joshua said calmly, rumpling the dark head before moving down the hall. Whatever his own anxieties about Jamie, he was evidently determined they wouldn't be communicated to his sons, his footsteps firm but unhurried as he mounted the stairs.

'Jamie's not very well,' Tommy explained gently to Clemency. 'An' my Daddy's going to go to the hospital to look after him. An' you're going to look after me,' he continued in case she wasn't quite clear on that point. 'An' I'm going to look after... I'll show you.' Tiptoeing towards the closed kitchen door, he beckoned over his small shoulder.

Clemency followed obediently, preparing herself to evince the right degree of surprise the moment she saw the kitten. In the event she had no need to pretend, her surprise and pleasure completely genuine as she saw the two occupants of the kitchen. Looking as if she had been in residence for years, the grey and white cat was sitting under the table, tail curled neatly around her paws, keeping a vigilant eye on her sleeping kitten.

'It was a nice surprise, wasn't it?' Tommy beamed with satisfaction at her reaction.

'Yes, it certainly was.' She smiled back, her ears tuned to the sound of activity in the hall. The ambulance must have arrived.

Dropping to his knees, Tommy crawled under the table. Though evidently tempted, he made no move to wake the kitten but, sitting back on his heels, studied the adult cat solemnly.

'Hello,' he addressed it politely, and paused, lifting his head as he too became aware of the alien noises in the house. Scrambling to his feet, he looked at Clemency uncertainly, and then his small face crumpled.

'It's all right, darling.' Stooping down, Clemency gathered him into her arms, hugging him close.

'I want to go with my Daddy and Jamie,' he mumbled fretfully, tears staining his cheeks.

'I know, darling,' she murmured softly.

Burying his face into her shoulder, his arms tightened around her neck as she carried him unprotestingly across to a chair.

Cradling him on her lap, she murmured to him soothingly, breaking off as the door opened and Joshua walked into the kitchen.

'How is he?' she asked quietly.

'Looking forward to riding in an ambulance.'

She didn't believe him for a moment, knew the words were solely intended to comfort Tommy, guessed from the shadows in his eyes that Jamie was still very much in pain.

'Coming to say goodbye to Jamie?' The studied casualness in Joshua's voice was belied by the muscle flickering along his lean jaw as his eyes rested on his small, tearful son.

'No.' Tommy buried his face against Clemency's shoulder again.

Making no attempt either to coax or pressurise Tommy into changing his mind, Joshua moved across the floor.

'The doctors at the hospital will make Jamie feel better,' he said softly, rumpling the small dark head.

Tommy didn't say anything but Clemency felt him relax slightly in her arms.

'Help yourself to anything you want, Clemency.' The blue eyes sought and held her grey ones for a brief second and then he turned towards the door. 'See you later.'

'Daddy?' Tommy lifted his head, his voice agitated. 'Have you got Hedgey?'

'Hedgey's with Jamie,' Joshua reassured him.

Tommy's face cleared slightly. He watched his father leave the room, stiffened as he heard the front door close a few moments later, and then nestled back against Clemency.

The kitten blinked open its eyes, stretched in perfect imitation of its mother, performed a whirling, energetic aerobic routine around the room, and then settled down to stalk a small pair of sandals.

Tommy surveyed the kitten with fascination but made no attempt to join it on the floor, seemingly content to remain in the warm security of Clemency's arms.

'Bed-time,' she said softly as his blue eyes began to haze over.

He nodded drowsily, slid off her lap and, slipping his hand into hers, led her upstairs to the room he shared with his brother. It must be the first time he's ever spent a night separated from Jamie, Clemency reflected as he snuggled down into his sheets.

'Shall I tell you a story?' he mumbled sleepily.

Wasn't that supposed to be her line? 'Yes, please.' Clemency sat down on the edge of the bed.

'Once upon a time,' he began in the best tradition, 'there was a snail.' He yawned. 'An' a caterpillar.' His

eyelids drooped. 'They were best friends. One day...'
On that cliff-hanger, he promptly fell asleep.

Tucking the bed clothes carefully around him,
Clemency very gently kissed his soft cheek and crossed
the room to draw the curtains. She left the door ajar and
made her way quietly downstairs.

Making herself a coffee, she carried it down the hall,
past a firmly closed door which she guessed was
Joshua's study and strictly out of bounds to his small
sons, and into the large, comfortably furnished sitting
room where the twins' presence was very much in evidence.

A column of assorted farm animals marched with
military precision along one skirting board. A completed
wooden jigsaw awaited admiration on the table by the
sash windows. In one corner work was in progress on a
construction of empty cereal packets and plastic cartons.

Clemency placed her coffee cup on a low table beside
the leather sofa and crossed the carpet, drawn to the
collection of framed photographs arrayed on top of one
of the bookshelves. Two small boys, in T-shirts and sun
hats, on a beach. One digging enthusiastically in the sand
with a blue spade. The other gazing down intently at a
shell in his hand, evidently hoping that the occupant was
still in residence and about to emerge.

Clemency smiled. It was not as impossible as she'd
supposed to tell the seemingly identical figures apart.

A more formal photograph of Tommy and Jamie with
their paternal grandparents, the likeness between the dis-
tinguished grey-haired man and his son very apparent.
It was as if she were seeing Joshua as he would look in
thirty years' time, the lines etched around the dark blue

eyes and firm mouth merely adding character to the compelling face.

Her eyes flicked to the next photograph. The twins with party hats on their small heads, about to blow out the candles on the birthday cake in front of them. Eight candles—four each. She jolted, and, picking up the frame, studied it more closely. Just visible in the background was a dark-haired young woman, laughing in the direction of the photographer. Anna.

Replacing the frame carefully back on the bookshelf, Clemency walked back across the room. She slipped off her shoes and stretched out on the sofa. The photograph had presumably been taken at Joshua's London home to which Anna had evidently been a welcome visitor, her presence at the twins' birthday party—very much a family occasion—indicating far more than a casual involvement in Joshua's life.

Clemency's eyes darkened; she was unhappily conscious of the tight sensation in her chest, the knotted feeling in the pit of her stomach. She'd assumed that Joshua's determination to keep their relationship strictly platonic arose from a disinclination to become involved with *any* woman. Her assumption had evidently been a wrong one.

Stretching out a hand, she picked up her coffee cup. Anna obviously lived locally. Had Joshua's decision to move down to Dorset been prompted by a desire to be closer not just to his parents, but Anna?

Pushing the uncomfortable thoughts firmly from her mind, she drained her cup and, swinging her legs to the floor, walked across the room to switch on the television, keeping the volume low so that she would hear Tommy should he wake.

Her eyes followed the figures on the screen, but when the credits came up she realised that she had no real recollection of the plot or characters of the film she'd just watched. Switching off the set, she left the room and made her way quietly back upstairs to check on Tommy.

He was still sound asleep, showed no signs of any restlessness, his arms stretched out above his head in peaceful abandonment. Her mouth curved as she gazed down at him. His features were barely formed, but already there was a decidedly determined thrust to his small chin.

She lifted her head, her heart squeezing as her eyes rested on the empty bed on the other side of the room.

'He's so little'. Joshua's gruff words reverberated in her head. Whatever she was feeling right now couldn't be compared to what Joshua must be enduring. Her concern for Jamie was the instinctive concern she would have felt for any child; Joshua's was the concern of a father for a much cherished son.

Silently she walked from the room. Just for that brief second on her doorstep, Joshua had looked so vulnerable, the expression in his eyes one she'd only ever witnessed once before. She bit her lip. And in that second she'd ached to reach out to him with the same unselfconsciousness she had over five years ago. But she'd been too inhibited, too constrained, and the moment had passed. Which, she reflected, was probably just as well.

Returning to the sitting room, she crossed to the window, stared out into the dusk for a moment and was about to draw the curtains when she saw the gleam of headlights coming down the lane. A few seconds later a taxi drew up in front of the house, discharging a shadowy, lean figure.

Flicking on the standard lamp as she passed it, Clemency hurried to open the front door, her eyes drawn questioningly to the blue ones as Joshua stepped into the hall.

'He's fine,' he said quietly, closing the door behind him. 'They're going to operate in the morning.' He followed her into the sitting room and sank down onto the sofa. 'Tommy?'

'Fast asleep when I last looked,' she reassured him. He looked completely drained, lines of weariness etched into his face.

'I'll come around first thing in the morning and get him ready for school,' she promised, guessing that Joshua would want to return to the hospital as early as possible.

'Thank you.'

She smiled, but avoided his eyes. Oh, God, she wished she had the right just to go over to him and put her arms around him. Just hold him.

'Goodnight.' She turned away swiftly and started for the door.

'Don't go yet,' he said quietly. 'Stay and have a coffee.'

She paused halfway across the room, and, turning round, surveyed him a little uncertainly. Was he reluctant to be left alone with his anxiety about Jamie? Somehow even under the circumstances she couldn't quite believe that this self-sufficient man would shy away from his own company.

'Oh, dammit!' he suddenly muttered. 'I must phone the paper.' A newspaper that would be minus a front page cartoon for the next few days, she guessed as he rose to his feet.

'I'll make the coffee,' she said easily. A coffee she didn't want. Any more, she thought as she returned to the room with two mugs, than she wanted to sit cosily beside Joshua on the sofa in the dimly lit room playing at 'just good neighbours'.

'Thanks.' He smiled up at her as she handed him a mug and joined him on the sofa.

'Beginning to stiffen up yet?' He turned to face her, leaning back against the arm rest.

'Just a little,' she admitted, aware of the tanned, muscled arm stretched out idly along the back behind her head. Increased familiarity with Joshua was most definitely not having the hoped-for effect. She took a sip of coffee, wondering if the ticking of the clock on the mantelpiece sounded as deafening to him as it did to her. She glanced up at him. His dark blue eyes were pensive, and it wasn't difficult to guess where his thoughts lay.

'Do you think I should get married again for the sake of the twins?' He broke the silence abruptly.

What? She almost dropped her mug of coffee, wondering if she'd misheard him as her eyes searched his face.

'Get married simply to provide the boys with a substitute mother?' Was this the same man she'd overheard such a short time ago declaring his household a male-only zone? 'Surely you're not serious?'

'Why not?' he enquired.

'Because it's ridiculous,' she said flatly. 'And would be totally unfair on the woman involved. Assuming any woman would be idiotic enough even to contemplate

such a proposition.' She didn't want to be having this
absurd conversation, although she had a fair idea of what
had prompted it. He'd been torn in two tonight between
the demands of both his sons, but it was a situation that
single parents must face on numerous occasions, she reflected, and Joshua's remedy was drastic in the extreme.

A sudden ludicrous vision of Joshua methodically
making a short-list of suitable candidates before inviting
comments from the twins unfolded in her head. Would
Anna figure high on the list? She squashed the thought
swiftly.

'Who would select the lucky winner—you or the
boys?' She absolutely refused to take this seriously.

'I would have the casting vote, naturally.' The solem-
nity in his face was belied by the glint in his eyes as
they locked briefly into hers. Had she been overreacting
to what had merely been a flippant question in the first
place?

Simultaneously they turned their heads as they heard
the scuffle of small feet coming down the hall. The next
second a tousled-headed small figure padded into the
room.

'It's me.' He beamed at them.

'Yes, I can see it's you,' Joshua drawled dryly.

'Where's Jamie?'

'He's staying at the hospital tonight.'

'To sleep?' Tommy frowned and scrambled onto
Clemency's lap, leaning back against her as he surveyed
his father.

'Yes,' Joshua returned casually. 'Which is what you
should be doing right now,' he added firmly.

'S'pose so,' he agreed reluctantly. 'G'night,
Clemency.' He hesitated and then very shyly bestowed

a tiny kiss on her cheek. 'What are those little spot things on your nose called?' He frowned. 'I forget.'

'Freckles.' Clemency tried to keep her face straight as Tommy inspected her with large, earnest eyes. Little spot things?

'Freckles,' he repeated obediently. 'They're quite nice, aren't they, Daddy?'

'Very nice,' Joshua agreed solemnly, rising to his feet. The blue eyes flickered with undisguised amusement over Clemency's somewhat disconcerted face.

'You can kiss me back if you want,' Tommy informed her bashfully.

'Thank you,' she said gravely, very conscious of the honour being bestowed upon her. She dropped a light kiss on top of his dark head.

He beamed and then suddenly flung his arms round her neck, hugged her fiercely and scrambled off her lap.

'See you,' he said nonchalantly, flapping a small hand as Joshua shepherded him from the room.

'See you,' Clemency returned, flapping a hand back. He had reassured himself that his father was back home; she doubted whether he would wake up again now. Muffling a yawn, she leant back on the sofa and smiled. It would be all too easy to get very fond of the small boy, she reflected, her thoughts, that had turned instantly to Tommy's equally endearing brother, interrupted by the peal of the telephone.

'Could you get that, please?' Joshua called from the landing. 'I'll be down in a moment.'

Rising to her feet, Clemency crossed to the small table and, picking up the telephone, reeled off the number written on it.

'Clemency? It's Anna. We met at lunch-time.'

'Yes, of course,' Clemency responded swiftly, registering with surprise that the other woman had evidently been *expecting* her to answer Joshua's telephone.

'I've just got home and found Josh's message on the answer machine. Is he still at the hospital with Jamie?'

'No, he's...' she glanced up '...just walked into the room. Hold on.' She held the receiver out as Joshua crossed towards her, his eyebrows raised enquiringly. 'Anna.'

'Thanks,' he murmured. 'Hello, Anna...no...tomorrow...yes, possibly.'

Feeling acutely uncomfortable eavesdropping, even though it was hardly her fault, Clemency walked over to the sofa, picked up the empty cups and headed for the kitchen.

Joshua had evidently called Anna from the hospital. Or maybe even earlier. Shrugging, she dumped the cups in the sink. She'd been under no illusions as to why Joshua had sought her own assistance tonight—expediency. Had his parents—now presumably in Canada—or Anna been available, she doubted it would have even occurred to him to turn to her for help. She frowned, staring out of the kitchen window into the dark garden, wondering why on earth it should matter anyway.

She'd completely forgotten the cats, started as she heard the cat flap swing open. Oh, heavens. Her eyes widened with horror. The grey and white cat had evidently been hunting and was bringing her trophy home, something small and furry and very much alive clutched in her mouth.

Instinctively she started to back across the kitchen, and then grinned foolishly as realisation dawned on her.

'It's only the kitten, you idiot,' she rebuked herself

out loud, and, sensing she was being observed, spun round and saw Joshua blocking the open doorway.

'Oh, Clemmy,' he laughed softly, shaking his head and then, taking two rapid strides, caught her up in his arms and hugged her.

Releasing her swiftly, he frowned slightly as if he was as surprised by his action as she was, and then slowly he began to grin.

Her face flushed, Clemency grinned back up at him. There had been nothing remotely sexual about the brief hug. It had been as spontaneous as Tommy's, and somehow that only served to intensify the warm pleasure tingling through her.

'Ouch, that's my leg not a climbing frame!' Stooping down, she carefully extracted the tiny claws from her jeans and placed the kitten gently on the floor.

'Why did you decide to go back for the mother?' she asked as Joshua ushered them into the hall.

He shrugged carelessly and then confessed. 'The kitten wouldn't stop crying for her.'

Smiling, Clemency's luminous eyes moved over the hard, tenacious profile. He would hate witnessing the distress of anything smaller and weaker than himself, she mused, especially when the remedy to ease the suffering lay within his power. She'd observed his male protectiveness towards his sons, had experienced it once herself.

Opening the front door, he walked her to the end of his drive, from where he had a clear view of her cottage.

'Would you like me to come round and help Tommy get ready for school in the morning?' Clemency offered.

'Oh, yes, please. I'd like to go to the hospital early to see Jamie. This is really kind of you, Clemency, I appreciate it. By the way,' he drawled casually, 'there was no need to beat a tactful retreat just now. Anna is Laura's sister. The twins' aunt.'

His ex sister-in-law. Practically a relative. Disturbed by the relief sweeping over her, Clemency was grateful for the darkness that concealed her tell-tale expression from Joshua's all too observant eyes.

'Goodnight.' She looked up at his shadowy face, wondering what had suddenly prompted him to clarify his relationship with Anna. Why on earth hadn't he introduced her as his ex sister-in-law in the first place instead of allowing her to jump to all sorts of conclusions? Retaliation for David? That would be adolescent in the extreme—and shamefully satisfying if it was true.

'Goodnight, Clemency.' Very gently he lifted a hand and touched her face. 'And thanks,' he added quietly.

It was the briefest of caresses but the warmth it produced stayed with her all the way up her own drive. She didn't look back over her shoulder but knew without doubt that Joshua would remain watching until he saw her disappear safely into her own home.

It wasn't until she'd closed the door behind her that she realised that her clothes and hair were damp. A glance out of the hall window confirmed that it was drizzling with rain. Odd, she hadn't noticed before. Although neither apparently had Joshua.

A large envelope tucked importantly in his arms, Tommy greeted Clemency enthusiastically outside the school gates the following afternoon.

'We made Jamie a special card today. Do you want to see?'

'I'd love to.' The rain had cleared up overnight, but

Friday had dawned much cooler, a brisk wind keeping the temperature down, and she'd temporarily abandoned her summer clothes in favour of jeans and a cream cotton sweater. 'Shall I take your lunch box?'

'Mmm.' He handed it to her, adding gravely, 'Thank you for making my sandwiches this morning.'

'My pleasure.' Joshua, his drawn face indicating just how little he'd slept, had left for the hospital while she had been still preparing Tommy's breakfast.

'My daddy always puts in an apple, too,' Tommy said gently as he carefully extracted the card from the envelope.

I know you did your best but perhaps if you could remember next time, please? Hiding her grin, she admired the card and handed it back to him.

With any luck he would be able to deliver it to Jamie in person tomorrow. Joshua had telephoned late morning, the relief in his deep voice unmistakable as he'd explained that Jamie's operation had been a complete success and that he was waiting for him to come round from the anaesthetic.

She relayed the good news to Tommy as they began walking homeward. He made no comment but, making a little whinnying sound, started cantering along the grass verge in front of her, breaking into a gallop as he saw the lean figure, striding to meet them.

'Daddy!' He flung himself against his father.

Clemency was able to resist the temptation to emulate him, but could do nothing to stop the rush of pleasure tingling through her as Joshua gave her a lazy smile above Tommy's head. A smile that told her all she needed to know about Jamie's welfare.

Tommy fished out the card again for further admiration and then, handing it to Joshua for safe keeping, slid one hand in his father's and the other in Clemency's. Three abreast, they sauntered along, discussing various names for the newest members of the Harrington household, although it went without saying that the official naming ceremony would be delayed until Jamie's return from hospital.

'I'd like to pop back to the hospital for a while this evening,' Joshua murmured to her as they exchanged conspiratorial grins at one of Tommy's more bizarre offerings. 'If you...'

'Of course,' Clemency said swiftly, gently releasing the small hand as they approached her gate. 'See you later.' As she encompassed both Joshua and Tommy with her warm smile, she was taken aback by the look of surprise on both their faces.

'I thought you were coming back to *my* house,' Tommy blurted out with disappointment. 'Daddy?' He looked up at his father.

'I expect Clemency has things to do,' Joshua drawled.

'Have you?' Tommy asked sadly.

'Well...not really.' Too late she saw the swift exchange between father and son and the next moment firm fingers folded around her right elbow whilst a small hand trapped her left palm.

Ignoring her laughing protests, her two male guards escorted her briskly past her cottage and up the adjoining drive. The senior guard released her arm whilst he fished in the pocket of his jeans for the door key, but his junior kept a firm clasp on her hand until she was safely inside the house.

*   *   *

'I thought I'd pick up a couple of takeaways on the way back from the hospital.'

In the process of running Tommy's bath, Clemency looked up as Joshua stuck his dark head around the door of the bathroom.

He'd disappeared for a swift shower while she'd been supervising Tommy's tea and had evidently taken the opportunity to shave as well, the dark five o'clock shadow around his jaw no longer in evidence.

'Any preferences?' Laughing softly, he broke off and crossed the tiled floor towards her. 'You've still got leaves in your hair.' Stretching out a hand, he brushed the tumble of red curls.

Her scalp tingling, Clemency smiled up happily into the warm dark blue pools.

'And a scratch on your cheek,' he added. Shaking his head as if she were a wayward child, he traced the tiny weal on her cheek.

'Battle scars,' she grinned, her stomach lurching. She must look as if she'd been dragged through a hedge backwards—which was almost quite literally the case. Much against her better judgement, she'd been persuaded by Tommy to go hunting for wolves in the thick undergrowth at the bottom of the garden.

'Pizza,' she murmured absently, breathing in the familiar clean, soapy scent of his skin.

'Any topping you dislike?'

'I keep forgetting to bring your sweatshirt round,' she remembered out loud, and saw the slight puzzlement in his eyes as if he couldn't for the life of him figure out how her mind had leapt from pizzas to sweatshirts. 'You left it on Monday. I don't like anchovies much.' But she loved the way his hair waved endearingly across his forehead when it was damp. Loved? Liked, she amended swiftly.

'No peppers,' Joshua murmured as he turned towards the door.

'No anchovies,' she corrected mildly. Hardly surprising his thoughts were elsewhere at the moment. 'Give my love to Jamie.'

He nodded and, whistling softly under his breath, strode out onto the landing. Recognising the popular tune, Clemency began humming the melody as she turned off the taps. She dipped a hand in the water to check the temperature and caught a glimpse of her reflection in the mirror above the wash basin as she straightened up. Was that girl with the flushed cheeks and inane grin really her? She laughed out loud and went in search of Tommy. Hunting for wolves must evidently agree with her.

It also apparently wore out small boys; Tommy practically fell asleep in the bath a little later.

'Goodnight.' She kissed him gently on the forehead as she tucked him up in bed.

'I'll tell you another story about the caterpillar an' snail tomorrow night,' he mumbled drowsily.

'I'll look forward to it,' she said softly as his eyes closed. Looking down at the sleeping boy for a long minute, she started to turn away and then faltered, it only then dawning on her with an uncomfortable little jolt that, like Tommy, she too had made the automatic assumption that she would be here tomorrow night.

An assumption that could very well be a false one. It was Saturday tomorrow, no school, and, now Jamie was convalescing, Tommy would probably start accompanying his father to the hospital. Naturally she would do everything within her power to help Joshua until Jamie was fully recuperated, but her current degree of involvement in the Harrington family was inevitably coming to an end. And next week she would be returning to work anyway.

Of course she'd still see Tommy and Jamie from time to time, but it wouldn't be the same, she mused sadly. Her gaze dropped back to the small child. She shouldn't be allowing herself to get so attached to him, she thought unhappily. Very gently she stroked back the dark lock of hair that curled over his forehead, her stomach muscles constricting. He looked so much like his father...

CHAPTER SEVEN

'PIZZA. No anchovies.' Joshua dropped two insulated round containers on top of the kitchen table and, shrugging his jacket from his broad shoulders, tossed it over the back of a chair.

'How's Jamie?' Clemency extracted two sets of cutlery from a drawer.

'Wide awake when I arrived—sore, but extremely proud of his stitches.' Opening the fridge door, he retrieved a bottle of wine. 'And eager to know every gory detail of his operation,' he added dryly.

Clemency smiled, imagining it, and conscious of the growing dusk switched on the overhead light.

'I thought we could eat on trays in the sitting room,' he said idly.

'I always find it a bit awkward,' Clemency returned casually, keeping her back to him as she began setting the table. Much safer out here in the brightly illuminated kitchen.

'Wine?'

'No, thanks,' she said firmly.

'Is something the matter?' he asked quietly.

She tensed as he came up behind her. 'Just a bit tired,' she said lightly, avoiding the far too perceptive blue eyes as she glanced over her shoulder. 'May I change my mind and have a glass of wine after all, please?'

'Of course,' he said courteously, but he didn't move away immediately, his eyes moving slowly over her face. For a moment she thought he was going to pursue the matter but he seemed to change his mind, and to her relief turned to reach up into the cupboard for another glass.

How would he react if she told him the truth, a truth she'd only just acknowledged herself? *Actually, Joshua. I think I'm falling in love with you.* There—she'd actually admitted it.

He would be alarmed, of course. And horrified. He would also be kind, considerate, gentle, hating to hurt her—ironic, considering it was those very attributes that made her love him. And it would be utterly unbearable.

Unobserved her eyes moved over the rugged contours of his face as he deftly uncorked the bottle of wine, the sum total of those aggressively male features utterly devastating. Why did the contents have to match up to the packaging? she wondered wryly. Why did her memories of him from five years ago, instead of being gilded by the passage of time, have to be so accurate?

She blanked her thoughts as he turned round and handed her a glass of wine.

'Thanks.' She took a sip, glancing out of the window. 'Josh!' Unthinkingly she clutched at his arm as her disbelieving eyes saw the grey shadow moving across the lawn. 'Look. I think it's a...'

'Badger,' Joshua finished softly as he followed her gaze, and, stretching out a long arm, flicked off the light.

It was much easier to see out now, the stout broad-bodied shape unmistakable.

Her mouth curving with delight, Clemency watched, transfixed, as the badger raised its snout, sniffed the air and then, seemingly untroubled by any alien scents, proceeded towards the dense undergrowth.

'Tommy would love it,' she breathed, turning to smile at Joshua. He wasn't looking at the badger; his eyes, almost black in the fading light, were focused with heart-stopping intensity on her face.

'Are you sure you want me to go and wake him?' he said gruffly, a muscle flickering along his jaw.

Her throat went dry at the expression in his eyes. Her hand, now frozen into immobility, was still resting on his bare arm and she could feel the hard band of muscles tautening beneath her palm.

Without taking his eyes from her face, he prised the wineglass from her other hand, setting it down on the counter. Then, raising her hand to his mouth, touched each finger in turn with his lips.

'The p-pizzas will be getting c-cold,' Clemency mumbled, every nerve-ending in her body seduced by warm, mesmerising pleasure. She should put a stop to this right now, move away.

'Yes,' Joshua agreed huskily, his fingers tightening around hers as he drew her unresistingly towards him. His other hand curved around the back of her head, his fingers sliding through her soft curls, tilting her face upwards.

Slowly and deliberately he lowered his head, his mouth brushing her throat, trailing a slow, sensuous path to her ear, teasing the delicate whorls with an expert tongue.

Eyes closed, Clemency swayed against him. She couldn't think straight any more, could hardly breathe, her heart hammering against her ribcage. Her arms crept up around his neck, drawing his head down towards her, relief shuddering through her as his mouth finally took possession of hers.

His lips moved searchingly against hers, exploring, tasting, tiny shivers tingling down Clemency's spine as his hands swept caressingly down the length of her body. His kiss deepened, became more demanding, charged with a fierce urgency as he crushed her against him, moulding her hips into the hard thrust of his thighs.

'Clemency...' His voice was hoarse and strained as he lifted his head. 'I want to make love to you.' His dilated eyes were half-closed.

But. 'I know,' she said huskily. She couldn't bear him to say the words out loud again, would say them herself... 'No strings. No commitment.' But she didn't care. Reality. Sanity. They would come tumbling back tomorrow. Tonight nothing in the world mattered but the here and now, the driving, aching need inside her—and Joshua. Most of all Joshua.

She almost cried out her protest as she felt his hold on her relax, his arms falling to his side. Uncomprehendingly she watched, rooted to the spot as he walked towards the door, his back rigid with tension. He must have seen the acquiescence in her eyes, must know...

Slowly he turned round and held out a hand, his eyes locking with hers across the shadowed room.

She drew in a ragged breath. The point of no return. He was giving her a chance to change her mind, wanted her to go to him freely and willingly without any coercion. The blood pounded in her head. No strings. No commitments. And no regrets.

Like a sleepwalker she moved towards him and took his hand. For a long minute he looked down at her, his breathing as erratic as her own, and then, his mouth descending on hers, swept her effortlessly up in his arms.

'Daddy?' The sleepy little voice drifted out onto the landing as Joshua carried her past the open door. She felt him tense, his eyes closing in momentary disbelief, and then as they flicked open saw a reflection of her own suppressed laughter. Sprung!

Placing her down gently on the carpet, he raised his hands in a gesture of helplessness and turned into Tommy's room. Concealed by the shadows, Clemency listened to his deep, soothing voice and the drowsy responses. She smiled, her heart constricting. All was well with Tommy's small world. His father was home.

I love him. Weakly, Clemency leant back against the landing wall for support, the intensity of the searing emotion knocking the breath from her body. I love him.

She pulled herself away from the wall and forced her trembling legs to carry her on down the landing, glancing through the open doors each side of her until she reached the final one.

She flicked on the switch by the door, the king-sized bed that dominated the room instantly bathed in a soft, mellow light. The blood moving like treacle in her veins, Clemency crossed the carpet towards it, staring at the indented pillow in the centre.

'Clemency?' She turned round, drawing in an unsteady breath as Joshua crossed the carpet towards her, a warm, melting ache tearing through her, loving him, wanting him so much.

Wordlessly, he took her in his arms, and the next moment she was kissing him back with the same fierce urgency as he was her. She could hardly breathe, let alone think, as he propelled her backwards onto the bed, drawing her against the hard length of his body as he stretched out beside her, his knowing hands moving intimately over her slender curves.

She offered no resistance as he eased the sweater over her head, shivering with shocked delight as his hands touched her bare, heated skin, moved in sensuous, feathery circles over her ribcage before closing with tantalising slowness over her breasts.

She sighed, her fingers curling through the thick dark hair as his lips took the place of his hands, his tongue flicking teasingly over the throbbing, aching peaks before drawing them into the warm moistness of his mouth. Senses reeling, she fumbled at the buttons of his shirt, intoxicated by the hard male skin beneath her palms as they slid over his muscled back.

His mouth moved across the soft silkiness of her stomach to the waistband of her jeans. She heard the rasp of the zip and wound her arms around his head, raising her hips as he eased the denims over her long, silky legs, gasping as his fingers slid beneath the lace briefs.

'Joshua,' she mumbled beseechingly, the teasing build-up of anticipation almost unbearable.

Her mouth went dry as he swiftly removed his own clothes, her eyes travelling over the wide, powerful shoulders, the flat stomach and strong thighs. Tentatively and then with growing assurance she began to explore the hard, taut lines, touching him, tasting him, breathing in the male scent of him, wanting to give him as much pleasure as he was giving her.

'Clemency, have you any idea of what you're doing to me?' he muttered hoarsely as her mouth closed over his warm skin. 'I wanted to take this so slowly, but I don't think I can wait any longer.'

With a muffled groan, he lowered himself between her thighs, supporting his weight on his forearms as his mouth claimed hers. Instinctively she started to move against him, her arms tightening around his neck, welcoming the urgent demands of his body.

Joshua's body. Fusing into hers. Dominating and teasing in turn. Delighting her. Driving her with him to a peak of pleasure so exquisite, so intense that she sobbed his name out loud as she spiralled with him, out of control, over the edge.

Slowly she opened her eyes, her erratic breathing returning to somewhere near normal as she tenderly stroked the back of the dark head pressed against her breast. Flooded with a glorious, warm lassitude, she smiled down at him, revelling in the weight of the satiated male body against her.

Nothing in her short-lived marriage had prepared her for this feeling of complete and utter well-being.

Joshua stirred against her, moving away onto his side.

'Hello, you,' he said softly, easing himself onto an elbow to look down at her. Gently he smoothed back the damp tendrils of hair from her forehead.

'Hello,' she returned with an idiotic grin, happiness soaring through her.

Kissing her softly on her lips, he rolled over onto his back and pulled her into the crook of his arm. Soporific warmth tingling through her, she nestled against him, her fingers caressing the tenacious jaw on a level with her eyes.

I love you. She hugged the words to herself, lost in a cocoon of complete unreality. Nothing in the world mattered but this moment in time, lying beside Joshua, touching him, listening to the sound of his rhythmic breathing. She wanted to saturate her senses with him, lock up some part of him inside her for ever.

'What are you thinking about?' Joshua asked softly, turning his head to smile down at her.

Smiling back, she shook her head slightly.

'No regrets?' he persisted.

'No,' she said quietly. At this moment, lying in the arms of the man she loved, filled with this wondrous feeling of completeness, how could she have any regrets? 'It was wonderful,' she said simply, tilting her face upwards. The most wonderful experience of her life. She grinned as she saw the flicker of male satisfaction in his eyes.

'Yes, it was,' he agreed.

Happiness spreading through her at the confirmation that the pleasure had been equally shared, she slid her fingers through his hair and, leaning over, kissed him on the mouth.

He smiled up at her lazily and touched her face, his fingers gently tracing the outline of her parted lips. Slowly he pulled her against him, his expert hands travelling languorously over her body, his gaze holding hers, watching the expression on her flushed face until, her breathing shallow, she closed her eyes and began to twist against him.

Stretching luxuriously, Clemency blinked open her eyes drowsily, her mouth instantly curving in a blissful smile as she gazed up at the ceiling, bathed in moonlight.

For a second, she lay perfectly still, savouring the feeling of perfect peace, and then slowly turned her head, disappointment washing over her as she discovered the empty pillow beside her. No sounds of activity from the *en suite* bathroom. Uncertainly, she studied the indented pillow and then her eyes jerked across the moonlit room as a shadowy, robed figure shouldered open the door, his two hands occupied with a tray.

'Breakfast,' Joshua announced, moving with silent, sure-footed grace across the carpet.

'At three in the morning?' Grinning, Clemency pulled the duvet up around her bare shoulders and sat up.

'I'm ravenous,' he confessed.

'So am I,' she realised happily, adrenalin tearing through her as she gazed up at him, loving him so much it hurt. She turned her attention to the tray as he placed it on the bedside table. He'd heated up the pizza and cut it into manageable slices. And gone out into the moonlit garden to pick a vase of late spring flowers. Her throat constricting, Clemency felt the tears prick her eyes as she studied the fragile blooms.

'Thank you,' she said huskily.

He didn't answer but, stooping down, framed her face with his palms and kissed her lingeringly on the lips. Then, moving round to the other side of the bed, he discarded his white robe, totally unselfconscious in his nakedness as he slid beneath the duvet beside her. But then why should he be embarrassed? Clemency thought with a lump in her throat, her eyes flicking over the lean, muscled torso as he propped himself up against a pillow. He was as beautiful, as magnificent as any sculpture.

He reached for a slice of pizza as she proffered the plate and then with his free hands drew her into the crook of his hard shoulder. Leaning back comfortably against him, Clemency took a bite from her own slice and grinned up at his shadowed face, the moon silvering the unruly dark hair.

'You look like a very disreputable highwayman.' She ran a finger across the stubble on his jaw.

'You've been acquainted with many?' he teased, tweaking her nose.

'Not many,' she conceded with a gurgle of laughter, wiping her fingers on a paper serviette. She could feel the heat of his body seeping through her skin, the brush of his long, hair-roughened legs against her own. She wriggled slightly, the duvet slipping down from her shoulders.

'Leave it,' Joshua commanded softly as she automatically started to pull it up again. Mesmerised by the dark gaze, she obeyed, heat scalding through her as his eyes dropped to the creamy swell of her breasts.

Stretching out a hand, he slowly eased the duvet down still further, exposing the taut, rosy tips.

'You're beautiful,' he muttered thickly.

Clemency released her breath in a long, shaky rush, the raw desire in his lingering gaze making the blood pound in her ears. Slowly, agonisingly, he lowered his mouth to hers, pushing her back against the pillow.

Dawn glimmered through the window when she woke for the second time, Joshua's sleeping body warm against hers, his arm draped possessively over her hips. Careful not to disturb him, she eased herself into a sitting position and looked down at him, caressing the familiar contours of his face with her eyes.

What would it be like to wake up in his bed every morning? she wondered wistfully. Dangerous ground, she reminded herself ruefully and, unable to resist, gently stroked back an errant lock of dark hair, smiling as he twitched slightly in his sleep. Muffling a yawn, she glanced at her wristwatch. It was so tempting to snuggle back down with him again, postpone reality for a short while longer but that could prove to be a fatal mistake should she fall asleep. The last thing she wanted was Tommy to bound into the room and find her curled up in bed with his father.

Easing herself out of the bed, she silently collected up her strewn clothes and dressed quickly. Joshua didn't stir, his breathing even and regular. Gazing down at him, she hesitated, loath to wake him and tell him she was going. He'd guess the reason, she was sure, and doubtlessly be relieved by her tactful departure.

Pressing a kiss to his forehead, she started for the door and then turned back, swiftly extracting a sprig of tiny blue flowers from the vase on the discarded tray. Not that she would ever need a reminder of last night. Giving Joshua one last, lingering look, she left the room, tiptoeing past Tommy's bedroom on her way downstairs.

She closed the front door softly behind her and stepped out into the early morning, taking a gulp of cool air into her lungs. She exhaled slowly, hugging her arms across her chest for warmth, but the chill beginning to seep through her was internal. This was reality. Slinking from Joshua's bed, from his home at dawn before his son awoke, because her presence might be an embarrassment. Because her presence was only a very temporary one.

She sighed softly. Joshua had exhibited warmth and tenderness as well as passion last night, but she didn't doubt for a moment that he was unselfish and experienced enough to make any woman feel special. It didn't mean anything, and she wasn't going to fall into the trap of kidding herself otherwise. Even at the most intense moment of their love making he hadn't said anything that had led her to suppose that they were sharing anything more than an enjoyable physical experience born out of liking, attraction, mutual need. Nor had he indicated that it was an experience he intended repeating.

Would she want that anyway? To pursue a casual affair with Joshua? Deluding herself all the time that she might make him fall in love with her while outwardly pretending she regarded their relationship in the same light-hearted spirit as himself? And when the relationship finished, as surely it would, what then? She shivered.

Please, she prayed, don't let me be that big a fool, don't let me take any more steps along that fateful road. She'd already taken one too many.

Clemency picked up the telephone for the third time, and for the third time she replaced it. She'd seen Joshua's car drawn up in his drive when she'd returned from her swift expedition to the village store for weekend provisions, knew that he'd been back from the hospital with Tommy for some while now. She bit her lip. Yesterday she wouldn't have hesitated in telephoning or calling round to get the latest progress report on Jamie.

But yesterday she hadn't spent the night in Joshua's bed. She walked back along the hall, through the sun-filled kitchen, out into the garden. Maybe he'd called round while she'd been out...?

'Hello, little one, what are you doing here?' She smiled down at the little black kitten that emerged from behind a large flowerpot. 'Exploring, hmm?'

No regrets. She slumped onto a wicker chair. So easy to claim that while she'd still been wrapped in Joshua's arms, still enveloped in that warm, hazy happiness. The kitten jumped onto her lap and began head-butting her chin. Perhaps, she thought wryly, if last night hadn't been quite so perfect, the sense of deflation today wouldn't be quite so acute.

Maybe he simply hadn't had a chance to telephone her yet. After all, he could hardly have a private conversation with Tommy within earshot. And, besides, he did have other things on his mind, she reminded herself guiltily. Like a small son in hospital. Absently she stroked the kitten. Purring ferociously, it curled up into a tight ball.

'Daddy, I've looked all over the garden and I can't find him anywhere.'

The anxious small voice carried clearly over the high garden fence.

'Don't worry, old chap, he'll come back when he's ready.'

Just the sound of the deep-timbred voice sent the adrenalin tearing through her, goose-bumps tingling down her stiffening spine. She could visualise so clearly the expression on the dark face as he looked down reassuringly at his small son.

'But what happens if he can't find his way home?'

There was an answering rumble but the words were indistinct as the voices faded away.

Galvanised into action, Clemency scooped up the kitten and approached the high fence, wondering why she hadn't reacted immediately.

'Tommy?' she called out, and was greeted by complete silence.

They must have retreated into the house. She looked down at the kitten and, sighing resignedly, started to make her way around the side of the cottage. It would doubtlessly return home in due course, but it was hardly fair to prolong Tommy's anxiety unnecessarily—just because she felt so ridiculously apprehensive about seeing Joshua. Her stomach was churning as if it were on a rollercoaster, her pulse racing as if she'd just completed a gruelling marathon...

She faltered as, peering over the front hedge, she saw the unknown second car drawn up beside Joshua's, and then, steeling herself, continued down her front path, her footsteps slowing again as the front door of the adjacent cottage opened and its owner strode out, followed by his son.

'I really don't want to go, Daddy.' Tommy was protesting without much hope as Joshua installed him in the back of the car before sliding into the driver's seat. The car started smoothly down the drive and then came to an abrupt halt as the occupants saw her.

Unfastening his seat belt, Tommy scrambled out of the car and came rushing down the drive towards her.

Carefully Clemency placed the wriggling kitten into the small, gentle hands. Rewarding her with a face-splitting grin, Tommy started back towards the house. 'Anna, Anna, Clemency's found him.'

Anna materialised on the doorstep, throwing Clemency a friendly smile before following Tommy as he scurried down the hall, presumably intent on reuniting the kitten with its mother.

'Hurry up, Tom.' Joshua stuck his dark head out of the window. 'Good morning, Clemency.'

Unconscious of the wariness in her eyes, she looked at him directly for the first time. He made no attempt to get out of the car to greet her. No warm, lazy smile of pleasure at her appearance. No acknowledgement of what had passed between them last night. No indication at all of what was going through that dark head.

'Good morning,' she returned evenly, her face a defensive, protective mask as she moved towards the car.

'Thanks for bringing the kitten home, but there was really no need. You're going to have a full-time job otherwise. Just shoo them away if either cat becomes a nuisance.'

Did he think she'd used the kitten as an excuse to come round and see him? Clemency's stomach muscles clenched. Did she now *need* an excuse to see him?

'How was Jamie this morning?' She hardly recognised her stilted tone. This was all wrong, she thought miserably. They shouldn't be looking at each other as if they were practically strangers.

'Fine,' he returned laconically.

'When will he be able to come home?'

'Early next week.' He paused. 'Thanks for all your help over the last couple of days.'

His words were as formally courteous as if she'd been no more than an acquaintance whose assistance he'd appreciated but no longer required. She wasn't sure what she'd expected from him this morning. Certainly not vows of undying devotion. But this impersonal casualness that bordered on indifference was incomprehensible, in what she knew of this man.

A creeping chill tingled down her spine. But what did she really know of this man? A woman who had been so easily deceived by her husband could hardly be termed an astute judge of character.

The chill intensified. Had she simply been swept up in a web of romanticism? Convinced herself she was in love with him when all she, too, had really felt was desire? Uncertainly she searched the blue depths, aware that she was being subjected to the same intense scrutiny, as if he too was seeking the answer to some unspecified, unspoken question.

Abruptly she broke his gaze as Tommy, chivvied along by Anna, came reluctantly towards the car.

'Got to have my hair cut,' he explained dolefully to Clemency.

'Have you?' she murmured sympathetically.

He smiled. 'And then when I come back I'm going swimming with Anna and Daddy. Will you come too?' Giving her no time to reply, he looked up confidently at his father. 'Daddy?' he said expectantly.

'Get in the car, please, Tom.'

'The more the merrier,' Anna contributed, smiling at Clemency.

'We want you to come with us, don't we, Daddy?' Tommy continued blithely, scrambling into his seat.

The silence was brief but marked and Clemency saw Anna frown slightly, her eyes puzzled as they rested on her ex brother-in-law, having evidently assumed, like Tommy, that he would automatically endorse the casual invitation.

'I expect Clemency has made other plans for this morning.' The finality in the deep voice was pronounced as Joshua leant over to check his son's safety belt. Lifting his head, his eyes trapped Clemency's. There was something unreadable in their depths but the underlying message couldn't have been spelt out more clearly. He had no wish for her company today.

'Have you?' Completely oblivious to the tension, Tommy looked at her with a crestfallen face.

'Yes,' Clemency said quietly, blanking her expression, recalling with painful clarity the almost identical scene yesterday afternoon, its happy, laughing conclusion so very different from today.

'Shan't be long.' The blue eyes flicked from Clemency to Anna as the car purred into life.

Motionless, Clemency watched it disappear down the lane. The coward. The unbelievable coward. He was terrified that she would start making assumptions about their relationship on the basis of what had clearly been nothing more than a one-night stand to him, terrified that she might start making some sort of emotional demands. So he was backing off completely.

She bit her lip. If last night had been so meaningless, why the warmth, the tenderness, the *flowers*? Why make her think he at least cared for her?

'Fancy a coffee?'

She frowned, realising with a jolt she had completely forgotten Anna. She was about to refuse when she saw the warm friendliness on the other girl's face, and changed her mind.

'Come and have one with me,' she suggested, and saw the brown eyes darken thoughtfully at the change of venue. Thoughtfulness that changed to outright speculation some minutes later as Anna instantly spotted Joshua's sweatshirt still strewn over the chair in Clemency's kitchen.

'Joshua left it here the other morning when he came to mend a window,' Clemency said swiftly, wondering why she was offering the explanation. 'Perhaps you could take it with you when you go?' she added casually. She certainly had no intentions of taking it around herself. In fact, in her present mood, she could cheerfully dump it in the bin.

'Sure,' Anna said obligingly, keeping up an easy flow of light conversation as Clemency made the coffee. Armed with a mug each, they moved outside and sat down on the loungers, exchanging swift grins as they saw the kitten padding determinedly up the garden. Reaching them, it sprang up onto Clemency's lap and settled down.

'Typical feline perverseness,' Anna commented. 'Tommy spent ages when we came back from the hospital trying to entice it onto his lap and it just ignored him completely.'

Clemency smiled. 'We'. She found Anna's casual use of the plural, the unity it implied, her evident inclusion in the trip to see Jamie, oddly unsettling.

'I know it's none of my business, but don't fall in love with him, Clemency.'

Clemency's eyes jerked to the other girl, caught completely off-guard by the softly spoken words. How on earth...? 'Is it that obvious?' she asked unsteadily.

'Only because I'm an expert on the subject.' Anna's mouth curved ruefully. 'Been there. Done that.' Her smile didn't quite reach her eyes. 'I had an awful schoolgirl crush on Josh when Laura first brought him home. I used to pray that he'd wait until I grew up and realise he'd chosen the wrong sister.'

'Maybe he did,' Clemency said quietly.

'No, it was always Laura. And I sometimes wonder if it still is,' Anna said evenly. 'It was she who instigated the divorce, not Josh. I think he hoped for a long time that they would eventually get back together again.'

With a dull ache Clemency remembered the number

of times Laura's name had crept into her conversation with Joshua. Were Anna's suspicions correct? Was he still in love with his ex-wife?

'I saw quite a lot of Joshua and the boys when he and Laura separated. He used to come and stay with his parents for weekends, holidays, and I went up to London occasionally.' She paused. 'We grew very close.' She saw the expression on Clemency's face and shook her head. 'Not physically. I wasn't a big enough idiot to go to bed with him.'

Clemency turned her head but it was too late; the warm rush of colour had betrayed her.

'Oh, Lord!' Anna clamped a hand to her mouth, and then slowly she began to grin. 'Lucky you. To be honest, I was never given the opportunity!'

Clemency's own mouth began to curve in response, and then the next second both girls were convulsed in laughter, their friendship sealed.

'Men!' Anna pulled a face as she sobered up, and then sighed. 'When you talk to Joshua, unlike so many people, he really *listens* to you, gives you his whole undivided attention, makes you feel just for a short time that you're the most important person in the world. And it's so easy to misread the signals, actually start imagining...'

'Yes,' Clemency said bleakly, knowing exactly what she meant.

'I made that mistake,' Anna confessed in a rush. 'For a while I really thought...' Her voice tailed off and she grinned. 'I know he's very fond of me—just like a damn big brother!'

Clemency smiled, guessing that despite her flippancy

Anna had been hurt, and quite suddenly she felt furious with Joshua on the other girl's behalf.

'Hey, it's not his fault,' Anna protested. 'It was all just wishful thinking on my part. He didn't give me any encouragement. Besides,' she said firmly, 'I'm over it now. Oh, heavens, I wish I hadn't started this conversation. I'm not in the habit of warning women off Joshua. And maybe your relationship with him is different.' She paused, looking uncomfortable. 'I'd just hate to see you get hurt.'

'I don't have a relationship with him as such,' Clemency said quietly. Joshua had made that painfully apparent this morning. Then, before she could help herself, asked, 'Have there been many other women since his divorce?'

Anna hesitated. 'I don't think he's been living like a monk exactly, but no one special.'

Physical rather than emotional involvements. Clemency studied her hands. No doubt with women who had been forewarned, as she had. No one could ever accuse Joshua of issuing false promises, she thought sardonically. But how many women, like Anna, like she herself, had woven little fantasies that they might be the one to make him forget the past? Forget Laura.

'What was—I mean what is—Laura like?' Once again she couldn't resist the temptation to voice the question in her head.

Anna frowned slightly. 'Clever. Ambitious. Very capable. She's not beautiful in the accepted sense but she's got something that makes men go weak-kneed and weak-headed at the sight of her. Sex appeal, I suppose,' she said thoughtfully. There was no trace of envy in her voice just an honest assessment. 'She's my sister and I love her,' she added slowly. 'But I'll never understand how she could have left Josh and the twins.'

It was, Clemency admitted silently, equally incomprehensible to her too. To be loved by Joshua, to be the mother of his children... She thrust the thought away from her instantly.

By unspoken agreement she and Anna changed the topic of conversation, chatting companionably about a wide range of subjects, discovering they shared many of the same interests as well as possessing a similar sense of humour.

'Sounds like Josh's car,' Anna murmured eventually. 'I could laze here all day.' She grinned and rose a little reluctantly to her feet. 'Why don't you come and have a meal with me one evening?' She issued the invitation with a warm smile as Clemency escorted her around the side of the cottage.

'I'd love to,' Clemency responded with pleasure, watching the brunette walk down the drive. However Joshua's circumstances might change in the future, she reflected with a shaming twinge of envy, Anna would always be a welcome part of his and the twins' lives. Whereas she was no more than a passing episode. The earlier burst of anger had long since faded. She felt empty inside as if she'd lost something infinitely precious, something that had never been hers in the first place. Something she wasn't even sure that she wanted any more.

Slowly she retraced her steps, her pace increasing as she heard the clamour of the telephone.

She recognised the voice of her superior at work immediately, her surprise that he should phone her at home on a Saturday changing to incredulity as she absorbed his words.

'You mean I've got the job?' she exclaimed. The much coveted post was actually hers?

'You'll hear officially next week but I thought I'd let you know off the record.'

'When do I actually start?'

'Two weeks.' There was the sound of rustling paper. 'I've got your itinerary for the next couple of months here. Three weeks in Paris. Then off to Milan for a fortnight. A week back in England. And then Sydney for four weeks.'

'Sydney?' Clemency repeated, a frisson of excitement tearing through her. She was going to Australia for a whole month.

'You'll get all the details next week. See you on Monday, Clemency. And congratulations.'

Clemency replaced the receiver, still reeling slightly from the shock. She ought to ring her mother and let her know. Later. When she'd had a chance to let the news really sink in herself.

She roused herself as the doorbell cut through her thoughts and went to answer it, her expression freezing as she saw the tall, lean figure standing on the doorstep.

'What do you want?' she said bluntly, and saw his eyes narrow as if he was surprised by her lack of welcome. What had he expected after his earlier brush-off?

'I thought you were going swimming.'

'Anna's taken Tommy on her own.'

She gazed up at him. Was that why he hadn't extended the invitation for her to accompany them? Because he'd wanted to use the opportunity to come and see her? Maybe she'd been too sensitive earlier, imagined slights that hadn't been intended.

'May I come in?' he said quietly. 'We need to talk.'

She hesitated for a moment and then turned away, leading him down the hall and into the sitting room, inviting him with studied politeness to sit down. The formality between them spoke volumes for the change in their relationship, she registered with a dull ache, as, refusing the invitation with equal courtesy, he moved across to the fireplace. He would never again wander into her house uninvited and unannounced.

'So what do you want to talk about?' she enquired coolly as he turned to face her. His recently trimmed hair was unnaturally disciplined, the rich waves subdued, sculptured to his well-shaped head.

'How about last night?' he answered dryly. Strong, tanned arms folded across his deep chest, his stance was self-assured, arrogantly masculine. Only the flickering muscle in the lean jaw, the guarded expression in the blue depths gave rise to the comforting suspicion that he wasn't finding this situation any easier than she was.

'Last night?' She hated the brittle, dismissive voice, hardly recognised it as her own. 'We're both adult. It happened.' Pride speaking, not her. Stupid pride.

'Just one of those things?' he said levelly.

'Well, wasn't it?' she challenged.

'No, it wasn't, and you damn well know it.'

'Why exactly are you here?' Her eyes blazed back into his as she rose jerkily to her feet. 'So that I can tell you just how wonderful you were last night? Do you want me to thank you?'

'Now you're being completely ridiculous.'

'I know.' She didn't feel remotely like laughing and

yet inexplicably her mouth was curving as she acknowledged the truth of his words. She was being absurd.

She saw his own mouth start to twitch, warmth dark-
ening his eyes as they held hers. Her stomach lurched.
She was so appallingly weak. If he walked over towards
her, pulled her into his arms she would sink into them
without protest. And it would solve nothing; the emptiness inside her would be assuaged only temporarily.

'I just want to forget last night,' she said in a rush. *I
don't want to lose you. I don't want to be just another
ex-lover.*

'You want to pretend it never happened? Block it out?
Like you tried to do with Simon and Lisa?'

She flinched, swinging round so that he couldn't see
her face.

'I'm sorry.' She felt his hand on her shoulder. 'That
was unpardonable.' He spun her slowly back towards
him. 'You can't just put the clock back, Clemency.' His
eyes moved slowly over her face, dropped to the curve
of her mouth. 'I can't,' he muttered. 'I don't damn well
want to.' His hand tightened on her shoulder.

'I don't want some meaningless, casual affair with
you.' She jerked herself free. Just the touch of his hand
and she could feel herself responding, her whole body
tautening, her resolve slipping. 'I don't want to creep
furtively from your bed every morning because of the
twins.'

'So that's why...' He frowned. 'Dammit all,
Clemency, do you think that's what I want either?'

'I don't know what you want,' she said flatly. 'I
haven't a clue what you're thinking. What you're feeling.'

'You want me to tell you I love you?'

Caught off-guard by his directness, she lowered her eyes instinctively, a warm rush of colour staining her cheeks.

'Because I can't,' he said quietly. 'I'm not offering you a lifetime guarantee and nor do I expect any similar assurances from you. That's a mistake I shall never make again.' A muscle clenched in his jaw and then relaxed. 'I enjoy being with you. And not just in bed. Although that is a definite bonus.'

She couldn't return his swift smile. And when she began to bore him? When her physical attraction lessened...?

'I care about you and would never do anything willingly to hurt you,' he said softly.

But he would hurt her. It was inevitable. He already had. Slowly she raised her eyes back to his. She loved him, but how much? Enough to risk it? Grab what happiness she could, however fleeting, knowing she would always be second best, and go hang tomorrow? Put her career on hold?

'Clemency?' he prompted softly.

'This is all hypothetical anyway,' she said evenly. 'I've just heard that my interview was successful.'

'I see.' The shutters slammed down over his eyes. 'Congratulations.'

'Thanks.' She'd never felt less like celebrating in her life. It had never occurred to him that she wouldn't accept the post. Any more than he would attempt to persuade her to change her mind.

'When do you start?' He began to walk out of the room, his expression and voice now completely controlled.

'I fly to Paris in two weeks.' *At least tell me you'll*

miss me. She followed him into the hall. 'Then I'm off to Milan and Australia.' Her earlier excitement had deserted her completely. She couldn't even inject a faked enthusiasm into her voice.

'I wish we'd just stayed friends,' she blurted out, looking up at him with wide, unhappy eyes as he paused on the threshold of the front door.

'We were never just that,' he said quietly.

'No.' It had always been there, the physical undercurrent between them. Last night hadn't just happened. It had been inevitable.

'Good luck.' Very gently he touched her face. 'And take care, hmm?'

'You too.' It was almost as if he was saying goodbye. Which was ridiculous, considering their proximity. It was inevitable that she would still see him from time to time when she was home. Bump into him in the village shop. Wave to him over the garden fence.

Her throat constricting, she watched him walk down the path. He was saying goodbye to what little they'd had together, knew, as she did, that nothing would ever be the same again. There was no going back. To all intents and purposes he was walking out of her life.

And she was standing there letting him.

CHAPTER EIGHT

'COMING to lunch, Clem? It's nearly two o'clock.'

Clemency glanced up from her desk as one of her colleagues walked into her office. She hadn't realised it was so late.

'I just want to finish off this report,' she murmured.

'Want me to bring you a sandwich back from the canteen? Egg mayonnaise?'

Clemency blanched, her stomach curdling, rebelling at the thought of food just as it had when she'd tried to eat breakfast that morning. 'No, thanks,' she said hastily.

'You look terrible. Even worse than you did first thing this morning.' The other woman studied Clemency's white face with concern.

'I do feel a bit queasy,' Clemency admitted.

'I hope you're not coming down with something just before you start your new post.'

'I'm probably just tired.' Last week had been frenetic and this one was proving to be almost equally so. Handing over to her successor. Last-minute preparations. Arranging for a married couple to come in once a week and clean the cottage and attend to the garden. Travelling up to London last Friday to meet the audit team who had just returned from three weeks in Geneva. The weekend spent with her parents, with whom she was going to stay again on Saturday night before flying out to Paris on Sunday with her new colleagues.

But her weariness owed far more to her restless nights

than the hectic days, Clemency admitted, her eyes dark-
ening unhappily. She could keep thoughts of Joshua at
bay during the day but at night it was impossible, the
image of his face, memories of the times they'd shared,
fragments of remembered conversations twisting in her
head as she stared up into the darkness.

It was nearly two weeks ago that she'd stood watching
him walk down the drive and out of her life. Twelve
long days, to be exact. Despite their proximity she'd
seen Joshua only once in that time, their cars crossing
in the lane. And then she'd been afforded no more than
a fleeting glimpse of a salutatory hand and two small
faces in the rear of the car.

She'd seized her courage and called him one evening
to enquire about Jamie, her genuine interest in the small
boy tempered by the overwhelming longing to hear the
sound of the deep-timbred voice. In the event the telephone had been answered by his mother who, after as-
suring her warmly that the convalescent was recovering
well, promised to tell Joshua that Clemency had called
when he returned. He hadn't called back. At least not to
her knowledge.

But then, she'd been home to do little more than sleep
the past days, returning late each evening long after the
twins would have gone to bed.

'I'm going to miss you, Clem. We all are.'

Clemency jolted, realising that for a second she'd
completely switched off to the other woman's continuing
presence in her office.

'I'll still be back from time to time.'

'But you'll be in a different department. It won't be
the same.'

'No,' Clemency agreed sadly, realising just how much

she was going to miss the colleagues with whom she'd worked for the past four and a half years. 'But I refuse to get maudlin today,' she said with a swift grin. 'I'll save that for tomorrow.' Her last day in this department. 'Anyway,' she continued, surveying her colleague with a warm smile. 'You're not going to be here yourself much longer.'

The fair-headed woman smiled back, smoothing down the voluminous smock she'd taken to wearing as soon as she'd learned that she was pregnant, and far earlier than was necessary. 'I'm beginning to show, aren't I?' she said happily.

Clemency nodded, smiling inwardly, the pregnancy still barely discernible.

'I've been so lucky, feeling as well as I do,' her colleague continued contentedly. 'My sister felt wretched for weeks at the beginning.'

'Did she?' Clemency said carefully, the innocent words suddenly sending goose-bumps prickling down her spine.

'See you later.'

As soon as the door closed, Clemency reached for her handbag and withdrew her personal diary, flicking back through the pages. Her hands suddenly clammy, she checked the dates again. There was no mistake. She was three days late.

She'd had so much on her mind lately she hadn't even noticed, hadn't even given it a thought until now. Pushing her chair back from the desk, she stared out of the office window. She'd been under a lot of emotional and physical pressure the last couple of weeks. It was hardly surprising if her normally very regular cycle was adrift. And that feeling of nausea with which she'd woken up this morning could be attributable to any number of things. Something she'd eaten yesterday. One of those twenty-four-hour gastric bugs.

She took a deep breath, trying to quell the upsurge of cramping panic. She couldn't *really* be pregnant, could she? Not after just one night? she blanked her face swiftly as her departmental head strode into the office, a file in his hand.

'Clemency, I wondered if you…? My God, you look dreadful,' he broke off abruptly. 'You should be in bed. I'll ask someone else to finish off that report. Go on home, and that's an order.'

'Thanks,' she said quietly. 'I will.' But first she needed to make a telephone call.

She waited until he'd left the office and then, her hand shaking, picked up the receiver. The earliest free appointment at her doctor's surgery, she discovered a few minutes later, was late tomorrow afternoon.

A short time later, battling against the wave of nausea creeping over her yet again, Clemency drove cautiously around the edge of the village green, keeping a vigilant eye on the crowd that had congregated to watch the activity centred around the large marquee as preparations for the supper dance the following night got under way. A team of men was ferrying trestle tables and chairs from a white van. Another team was busily erecting fairy lights.

Clemency barely noticed either of them. Joshua's baby growing inside her at this very minute. Could it really be true? Her stomach lurched, gagging bitterness rising in her throat. Oh, God, she was going to be sick.

A few agonisingly long seconds later she turned into her drive. Slamming on the brakes, she jumped out of

the car and sped into the house, leaving the front door
open behind her as she dived into the downstairs cloakroom, reaching it just in time as she retched into the
basin.

Her legs like jelly, she clutched the side of the basin,
waiting for the nausea to pass, waiting until she could
muster the strength to turn on the tap and wash her face.
Unable to remember when she'd ever felt so wretched,
she emerged unsteadily from the cloakroom, her legs
almost giving way completely as she saw the tall, lean
figure standing on the threshold of the open front door,
a parcel in one hand.

'Joshua, what are you doing here?' She reached for
the wall for support.

He didn't answer. Taking one look at her ashen face,
he deposited the parcel on the hall table, grasped hold
of her arm and guided her into the sitting room.

'Lie down,' he ordered, pushing her gently down onto
the chintz-covered settee.

Unprotestingly she obeyed, stretching out her legs and
leaning back against a cushion. Closing her eyes, she
willed her spinning head to clear, hardly aware that
Joshua had left the room until he returned with a glass
of water and the car rug that she'd left on one of the
kitchen chairs.

'Thanks,' she mumbled as he draped the rug over her.
She began to stop shivering, warmth slowly creeping
back through her body.

He was bending over her and for a second she forgot
everything, drinking in the familiar soapy scent of his
skin, aware of nothing but the rush of pleasure at just
seeing him. She wanted so badly to lift a hand and brush

back the errant lock of thick, dark hair that waved so endearingly across his forehead.

'Here.' He handed her the glass of water.

She took a sip, conscious of his eyes still focused intently on her face. God, she must look a mess.

'Feeling better?' he asked quietly. For a second she thought he was going to sit down beside her on the settee but then he seemed to change his mind and crossed to the armchair opposite her. She was both disappointed and relieved.

'Yes. I think so.' She wriggled into an upright position. 'I must have picked up some sort of bug,' she mumbled, and took another swift sip of water to ease her constricting throat, painfully imagining the scenario right now had only things been different. Had Joshua loved her, she would be at this very moment locked in his arms, joyfully telling him the news that they might be having a child.

'What are you doing here?' She voiced her earlier question again abruptly, suddenly desperately wanting him to be gone from her home while she was in this vulnerable state, terrified that she might be tempted to confide her suspicions to him. She shuddered inwardly, visualising the shocked horror on his face. He'd made love to her to satiate a physical need, not to create a new life.

'I brought around a parcel for you. The postman left it with me this morning,' he explained quietly.

He'd just been acting the good neighbour. 'It's probably my jacket,' she mumbled aloud. The one she'd bought and left to be altered when she'd gone up to London for her interview. Her chest tightened as she recalled with painful clarity the moment when she'd stepped off the train that evening and seen Joshua waiting for her. Barely two weeks ago, it seemed like a lifetime.

'How's Jamie?' she asked swiftly.

'Dying to get back to school with Tommy. My mother's with him at the moment. She's been over most days.' He paused, his mouth twitching. 'I've been reliably informed by Jamie that his grandmother's cooking is infinitely better for invalids than mine.'

She hardly heard his words, fascinated as always by the way the corners of the firm mouth curved when he smiled. Suddenly aware that he had stopped speaking, she lifted her eyes, unnerved to discover that he was surveying her with the same intensity.

'I must go and pick Tommy up from school, and you should be in bed.' Breaking the tense, protracted silence, Joshua rose abruptly to his feet. 'Is there anything I can get you before I go?' He moved over to the settee and looked down at her.

She shook her head. 'I don't think so, thanks.' Her expression and her voice were as carefully controlled as his.

'I'll see myself out,' he said quietly. 'Go to bed,' he advised firmly, and, catching her completely off-guard, unexpectedly stretched out a hand and gently ruffled her hair. Then, without witnessing the surprise on her face, he strode from the room. A few seconds later she heard the front door close quietly.

Her scalp tingling from the fleeting touch of his fingers, she swung her legs to the ground, the weakness in her limbs not solely attributable to the queasiness beginning to envelop her again.

Starting to shiver, she made her way upstairs, pulled

the curtains in her bedroom and lay down on the bed, wrapping the duvet around her. Despite her conviction to the contrary, sleep, that had eluded her for so many nights, claimed her almost immediately.

It was dark when she woke, momentarily disorientated by the discovery that she was lying in bed still fully clothed. Thirsty, she went downstairs, made a cup of herbal tea and then after undressing, returned to bed, falling into undisturbed slumber again almost immediately. She woke early on Friday morning, nausea free, and filled with a strange, inexplicable feeling of serenity, the latter sensation disintegrating the moment full consciousness returned.

Parking her car in the drive with considerably more finesse than she had the previous afternoon, Clemency gathered up the cardboard box from the passenger seat beside her. It contained not just the contents of her desk, but the cards and small humorous gifts she'd received from her colleagues at lunch-time when they'd gathered for a small, impromptu party to congratulate her on her promotion and wish her success in her new post. She'd been touched by their well-wishes, but it had been a considerable strain evincing a pretended enthusiasm for a post that no longer seemed remotely important to her and from which she might well be resigning in a few months.

She kicked off her shoes in the hall and padded upstairs to her bedroom. Hurriedly stripping off her suit, she showered and changed into a blue cotton dress, leaving her tanned legs bare. Moving across to the dressing table, she sat down and ran a comb through her silky red curls before applying a light touch of morale-boosting lip gloss. Oh, heavens, she'd cancelled her milk as from tomorrow but had forgotten to do the same for the newspaper.

She glanced at her wristwatch. If she hurried she'd have time to call into the village shop and rectify the omission before her appointment at the surgery. She closed her eyes for a second and, taking a long, calming breath, forced herself shakily to her feet.

'Off to Paris on Sunday?' The middle-aged woman smiled knowledgeably at Clemency across the counter as she settled her outstanding account.

'Yes,' Clemency smiled back, momentarily taken aback before remembering that the other woman was related to William. She'd paid a brief visit to the ex-gamekeeper and his wife last week to explain her future long absences from home. She'd been upset and startled by their distress at the news, hadn't realised until then just how fond they'd become of her. And she of them.

'Going on holiday?' a voice enquired, and she turned to smile at the young local vet waiting behind her with an evening paper in his hand. He'd come to her aid once when she'd had a flat tyre, and had followed it up with an invitation for a drink. She'd accepted but, sensing an interest she didn't return, had gently refused subsequent invitations.

Aware that her audience had increased, the queue of waiting customers eavesdropping unashamedly, she explained about her new job.

'Well, mind you save me a farewell dance tonight.' The vet grinned.

'I'm not sure if I'm going,' she said lightly, and recognised her gaffe immediately as she saw the faintly disapproving expressions on the faces around her. 'But probably,' she finished quickly. The dance was the biggest event in the village social calendar, involved a great deal of work by its voluntary organisers, and should be supported in person, she conceded, not merely by the token purchase of a ticket.

'Good. See you tonight, then.'

'Right,' she nodded. She could put in an appearance, needn't stay too long. She started for the door.

'Hello, Clemency.'

He towered over her, formidable and uncompromisingly male, blocking her exit.

'Hello, Joshua,' she returned weakly. The shop, the customers faded into a hazy background, all her senses focused on the lean figure.

'Feeling better?'

'Yes, thanks. I think it must just have been one of those twenty-four-hour bugs,' she added lightly. She saw his eyes flick from her face and followed their direction. Tommy and Jamie were standing by the confectionery display, evidently having been told that they could select a chocolate bar each as a treat. Simultaneously they turned round and came towards their father with their choice.

'Hello, Clemency.' Jamie beamed up at her.

Clemency smiled back. 'How are you?'

'I might be going back to school next week,' he informed her jubilantly. 'This one, please, Daddy.' As Jamie looked up at his father, Clemency turned to the other small boy.

'Hello, Tommy,' she said gently.

'Hello,' he returned after a moment's pause, dragging

the word out reluctantly. Refusing to look at her, he studied his shoes intently.

Clemency swallowed hard, her eyes on the bowed, unresponsive head. *I miss you, too, Tommy.*

'Better get in the queue, Daddy,' Jamie prattled happily. 'Can I give the lady the money, please?'

Joshua dug into the pocket of his jeans and produced some coins. Clutching them in his small hand, Jamie bustled importantly towards the counter.

Tommy suddenly raised his head. 'Why don't you come to my house any more?' he said abruptly.

Clemency looked at him with a feeling of utter helplessness. *Because I'm too much of a coward to take a chance on your daddy. Because he doesn't love me and I'm too scared of loving him, of loving both you and Jamie too much.*

'Why don't you like me any more?' he mumbled, shuffling his feet.

'Tommy, of course I still like you.' Clemency dropped to her haunches in front of him. 'Very, very much,' she said softly. 'And Jamie.'

The small face cleared slightly. 'Then why don't you come to see us any more?'

'I've been very busy.' She cursed silently the moment the words left her lips. Of all the insensitive, crass, stupid... But it was too late to retract the words; the damage had been done, Tommy withdrawing from her again.

'And now you're going away,' he said flatly.

'Not for ever,' she said swiftly. This was awful, and Joshua was no help at all. 'I shall be back from time to time.' Back to base. She couldn't look at Joshua, knew exactly what must be passing through his head, what memories she'd revived. *I'm not Laura,* she felt like

shouting. The situation is completely different. I'm not
your wife. I'm not the mother of your children. Oh, God.

'Are you all right?' She felt a pair of firm hands on
her arm, steadying her as she swayed dizzily to her feet.

'Yes, fine,' she muttered, the flash of concern in the
blue eyes, the fleeting touch of the lean fingers on her
bare skin suddenly unbearable. As unbearable in a different way as the accusation on Tommy's small face.
Murmuring something incoherent under her breath, she
headed blindly for the door.

She took a deep, controlling breath as she stepped
outside, and then hurried down the high street, turning
up a side street to the large Victorian house that had
been converted into the doctors' surgery.

The waiting room was half-full, and, giving her name
to the receptionist, she picked up a magazine and sank
into a vacant chair. The walk from the shop had been a
short one but she could feel the beads of perspiration
gathering on her forehead, the panic-stricken confusion
that she'd managed to control all day threatening to engulf her completely.

The words on the page blurring in front of her eyes,
she brushed a damp hand across her forehead, the unnatural warmth draining from her body as the door of
the surgery opened and three figures walked in.

Jamie spotted her immediately. 'Look, Daddy, there's
Clemency.'

Joshua turned his head, his dark eyebrows creasing
across his forehead in a sudden frown as his eyes flicked
over her, before moving towards the receptionist.
Tommy simply ignored her.

Releasing his father's hand, Jamie bounded towards
her. 'This is really funny, isn't it? You being here, too.'

'Yes,' Clemency returned weakly. Hilarious. Why hadn't she made an appointment at an anonymous city clinic?

'I'm going to have a check up on my wound,' he continued blithely. 'Do you want to see them?' Whipping up his T-shirt, he proudly exhibited the slightly puckered dark line across his lower abdomen.

Clemency made admiring noises that ended in a muffled choke as Joshua folded his frame into the chair on the other side of her, Tommy leaning back against his father's legs with his back very pointedly turned towards her.

'Hello, again.' She couldn't look at him. Did not dare look at him.

'Are you a bit poorly?' Jamie enquired sympathetically, standing in front of her.

She smiled vaguely. There is just a very faint possibility that I may be having your half-sister or -brother. She battled desperately against the burst of hysterical laughter as she sensed Joshua's gaze upon her. Colour flooded and then ebbed from her face. He couldn't possibly suspect, so why did she feel as if she was wearing a placard around her neck?

'Mrs Adams?' the receptionist called out.

Thankfully, Clemency rose to her feet, aware of three pairs of blue eyes following her jerky progress across the waiting room. When she reappeared some while later, Joshua and his two small sons had gone.

A baby. Clemency stared out of her bedroom window, watching the sinking sun, her fingers awkward as they fastened the gold chain around her slender neck, the opal pendant nestling on the creamy skin exposed by the flattering scoop of the soft, silky midnight-blue dress.

Joshua's baby. The weakening sensation spreading through her body made her reach for the support of the window still. *You don't know for certain. Not yet.* Not until tomorrow, the doctor having assured her that the results would be through first thing in the morning.

Her and Joshua's baby. Their child.

Slowly she moved away from the window, her eyes jerking to the alarm clock by her bed. In just over twelve hours she would know. Twelve long, unendurable hours.

Slipping her feet into the low-heeled strapped sandals, she picked up the ticket lying on her dressing table and placed it in her small clutch bag. Without much interest she gave herself a cursory glance in the mirror, wondering how on earth she could look so normal, her luminous grey eyes serene, her forehead smooth, uncreased by the anxiety gnawing away inside of her. Her whole life might well be about to change dramatically and she was calmly tripping off to the supper dance with apparently not a care in the world.

'Would you like a drink?'

'I'd love an orange juice.' Clemency smiled up at the young vet. He'd been standing just inside the marquee entrance when she'd arrived and had detached himself immediately from the group of people with whom he'd been chatting, greeting her with warm friendliness.

As he threaded his way towards the bar, set out beside the lavish buffet, Clemency's foot tapped unconsciously in time to the rhythm of the beat issuing from the band ensconced in the far corner, its mixed repertoire reflecting the wide range of ages and tastes amongst its audience.

The latest popular song gave way to a slower, familiar melody, and the energetic teenagers on the dance floor were joined by parents and grandparents. Clemency's eyes softened, tears suddenly pricking them as she spotted William and his wife amongst the throng. Almost unrecognisable in a formal dark suit, he was gazing down at the frail white-haired woman in his arms as if she was the most entrancing girl in the world.

'They've been married over fifty years,' the vet murmured, following her gaze as he rejoined her.

Already aware of that fact, Clemency nodded and took a swift sip from her glass to dislodge the lump in her throat. In her present emotionally volatile state she couldn't afford to start getting sentimental—might very well burst into tears.

'Hi, Clemency,' murmured a soft voice behind her.

'Hello, Anna.' Clemency turned to greet the brunette with pleasure, pleasure that changed to a flicker of apprehension as she automatically searched for an approaching dark head.

'I'm glad you're here,' Anna said warmly. 'I was dreading coming on my own and finding no one I knew,' she said cheerfully.

The assertion was unconvincing, and Clemency suspected that Anna was subtly informing her that she hadn't been escorted by her ex brother-in-law.

'I haven't seen Josh, have you?' Anna continued casually, confirming Clemency's suspicion. 'I know he was planning to come.'

'No,' Clemency returned with equal casualness. Was Anna warning her that Josh was bringing another partner with him so that she could prepare herself? Her stomach lurched.

'What a gorgeous dress,' she said brightly, deliberately changing the subject. Joshua had the perfect right to bring whomsoever he chose with him tonight. She had no claims on him or he on her. But, please, don't let him. Not tonight.

'What, this old thing?' Anna grinned, looking down at the obviously brand-new flame-coloured dress that suited her dark looks and slender figure to perfection.

'You look lovely,' Clemency said sincerely, a fact, she observed with wry amusement, that hadn't gone unnoticed by the young vet. Swiftly she made the introductions, saw the reciprocal spark of interest in Anna's eyes, interest that strengthened as the tentative, exploratory conversation between them became increasingly animated.

Clemency grinned inwardly as she saw the absorbed expressions on the faces of her two companions. She was definitely becoming superfluous to requirements, she decided without rancour. Murmuring something about going to say hello to William and his wife, she edged away and, glancing back over her shoulder, saw Anna, vivacious and happy, being led very purposefully onto the dance floor.

Spotting the elderly couple, she began to make her way towards them, exchanging greetings with various acquaintances as she eased her way through the congested marquee.

'Would you like to dance?' A youth, whom she recognised vaguely as the teenaged son of one of the local farmers, barred her way, blushing furiously.

Conscious that a group of his peers were observing

him with profound interest, Clemency didn't have the heart to refuse.

'Thank you. I'd love to,' she responded with a swift smile, and saw his hue deepen to an even deeper scarlet.

Holding her awkwardly, almost at arm's length, he began to shuffle her inexpertly around the floor.

'Sorry,' he stammered as his foot crushed one of hers.

'That's all right.' Clemency concealed her wince, and then felt the colour drain from her face as over her partner's shoulder she gazed straight into a pair of dark blue eyes.

There was a tiny flicker of acknowledgement and then he disappeared from her view, leaving her with only a fleeting impression of dark tailored trousers and a blue silk shirt. But the image of the small blonde woman in his arms was printed indelibly in her head.

He was only dancing with her, for heaven's sake. That was what people did at a dance, Clemency Adams, dance together. But rationality, all the logic in the world, did nothing to ease her cramping muscles that were knotted so fiercely that they actually physically hurt.

She forced her attention back to her partner, relieved when the tempo of the music changed and he released her awkwardly.

'Thank you,' she said kindly but firmly as he looked at her hesitatingly as if about to suggest they continue.

'Maybe later,' he suggested hopefully, and, seemingly satisfied with her noncommittal smile, returned to his group of friends, one of whom, evidently intent on emulating him, began to move towards Clemency.

She might have been amused at other times by her apparent popularity amongst the teenaged male populace of the village, but not tonight. She turned away swiftly, losing herself in the mêlée that was heading for the buffet as the band announced it was taking a short respite. She caught a glimpse of Anna, laughing up at the attentive man by her side, both of them oblivious to the plates in their hands. Then through a sudden gap she glimpsed Joshua, his hand folded lightly around his companion's elbow as he guided her towards the linen-covered trestle tables.

Swirling round, murmuring apologies as she collided with someone, she threaded her way back through the crowd towards the exit, the heat, the rising crescendo of exuberant voices unbearable. She took a deep breath as she emerged into the night air, welcoming the coolness on her skin. Slowly she started to walk around the perimeter of the marquee, her path illuminated by the string of fairy lights that adorned the surrounding trees. She would have to return inside in a moment to retrieve her jacket which she'd discarded earlier on one of the several coat stands that had formed the makeshift cloakroom.

Completing the circuit, she came to a halt, standing back in the shadows, watching the sudden stream of revellers that poured out of the marquee. Armed with plates and glasses, they distributed themselves amongst the tables and chairs set out on the grass.

Everyone belonged to a group, formed part of a couple. She gritted her teeth, a wave of loneliness swamping her. She recognised most of the faces by sight if not by name, knew perfectly well that she could walk out of the shadows, draw up a chair to any of the tables and she would be welcomed warmly.

But she had no desire to do so. She wanted to be with Joshua and no one else, wanted to be with him with an intensity that made her ache. She wanted to feel the warmth of his protective arms around her, wanted to see the dark blue eyes look down at her with the same expression she'd witnessed earlier in William's as he had gazed at his wife of half a century. She wanted a lifetime commitment, fifty years of Joshua's tomorrows.

Stop it. Just stop it, she ordered herself roughly, spinning away. She would collect her jacket in the morning, had no doubt that it wouldn't be the only one left behind. Shoulders hunched miserably, she set off into the night along the well-worn path across the green, the sound of voices, laughter, fading away behind her. The moon slid behind a cloud and she faltered, unease prickling down her spine. She hadn't realised quite how dark it was. No comforting lights issuing from the houses in the lane ahead, the occupants either in bed or at the dance.

Cautiously she moved on into the blackness and froze as she heard the sound of hurried footsteps behind her. She whirled round, just as the moon reappeared, illuminating the tall, loping figure.

'Joshua.' She was momentarily weak with relief and then furious. 'What the hell do you think you're doing, creeping up on me like this?'

His eyes blazed back into hers. 'Where exactly do you think you're going?'

'Home. Where did you think I was going? On some nocturnal ramble?'

'Why didn't you get a taxi? Ask someone for a lift?'

She opened her mouth and shut it, anger draining. He'd been concerned about her. 'It's perfectly safe,' she mumbled. It wasn't until a long time later that it occurred to her to wonder how he'd been aware of her stealthy departure in the first place.

'I'll walk with you the rest of the way,' he said abruptly.

'There's really no need,' she said stiffly, but knew she was only paying lip service to the words.

He ignored her as she guessed he would, shortening his strides to match hers.

She stole a sideways glance but his shadowed face was unreadable. He was so close, so tantalisingly close. She wished he would just reach out and take hold of her hand, had to clench her fists to stop herself taking the initiative.

'Won't your blonde friend be wondering where you've got to?' She could hardly believe that the snide, disparaging little voice breaking the silence had emanated from her. She hadn't actually said blonde bimbo but the implication was there, the pathetic little jibe hanging in the air between them.

'If you're referring to Kate,' he said evenly, 'she happens to be a solicitor and a very old friend. We were at school together.'

'She's a friend, just like we were friends?' she taunted, and ground to a halt. 'I'm sorry, Josh.' The words tumbled out in a miserable rush. He must dislike her at this moment as much as she did herself. 'I'm not normally so...bitchy.' She couldn't bear him not even to like her any more.

'You're not normally pregnant.'

She went rigid. How could he possibly...? 'You saw me in the surgery and you assume I'm pregnant?'

'The possibility started to cross my mind yesterday,' he said quietly. 'I didn't pick up on the obvious signs with Laura. It's not a mistake I'm likely to make a second time.'

'I've already told you, it was just a bug. And I could have been at the surgery for any number of reasons.' She couldn't carry it off, knew the truth was written all over her betraying face as the blue eyes locked with hers. 'It's just a very remote possibility,' she muttered.

Wordlessly he took hold of her arm and propelled her towards a bench overlooking the small duck pond. Releasing his hold, he sat down beside her.

'I should have been more careful, taken precautions,' he said quietly. 'But I suppose I assumed...'

'That I was on the pill,' she finished steadily.

He nodded and then shook his head. 'No, dammit. I simply didn't give it a thought at the time.'

'Nor did I,' she muttered.

'Were you going to tell me?' His voice was strained, unnatural, the bleakness in his eyes transporting her back more than five years. The situation, even the setting now, was so horribly similar, and yet there was one vital difference: he had been in love with Laura.

'Clemency?' he prompted gruffly as she remained silent.

She swallowed. 'I don't know,' she said finally.

'It didn't occur to you that I might actually be interested in the fact that you're carrying my child?'

'I don't know if I am.' He was talking as if it was a foregone conclusion. 'I won't have the result until tomorrow.'

'Assuming the result is positive?'

She didn't answer.

'I take it that you have actually thought about it, been making plans...' He trailed off, his eyes narrowing. 'My God, you've just blocked it out...'

'I haven't...' *Dared* think too much about the future. She slammed her mouth shut.

'Haven't had time to think about it?' he suggested, his voice cutting through her like a knife. 'Too busy preparing for your new job? Or have you simply refused to face the fact that the possibility might prove to be a very real, unwelcome actuality?'

Her hands tightened into small fists; for a moment she actually hated him, hated him for knowing so little about her. Joshua's baby unwelcome? She battled against the surge of tears springing to her eyes, wanting to laugh and cry at the same time. She hadn't dared start building up her hopes, making plans for the future, terrified of the disappointment should her suspicions fail to be confirmed. Joshua's son or daughter. Part of him that would always belong to her, part of him she could love unreservedly.

'I don't want anything from you,' she said unsteadily. 'This is my problem and I shall deal with it.' She regretted the choice of words the moment they left her lips, saw his mouth tighten. 'My responsibility,' she amended swiftly.

'Oh, no, Clemency,' he said ominously. 'Our responsibility. And I'm damned if I'm going to let any child of mine be brought up by a succession of nannies, packed off to boarding school at six, farmed out in the holidays.'

And he really thought that was what she would want for their child? 'I'm going home.' She forced the words through her stiff lips, jerking herself to her feet.

He caught up with her a few seconds later. 'That was unfair,' he said quietly.

'Yes,' she said dully, and shivered.

'Didn't you bring a jacket with you?'

'I left it behind. I'll pick it up tomorrow.'

He didn't speak again until they reached her doorstep, his thoughts no doubt as confused as her own. Fishing for her key in her bag, she looked up at him. 'Goodnight, Joshua.' *Please just take me in your arms and hold me. Hug me. Just for a moment.*

'Goodnight,' he returned quietly, his face a shadowed mask. He started to turn away and stopped.

'Clemency,' he said slowly, looking down into her upturned face, 'if—'

'I won't marry you,' she cut in bluntly.

'I don't recall asking you.' Inexplicably his lips twitched at her forthrightness.

'But you were about to,' she said with quiet certainty. 'Make the honourable offer.' She forced the flippant lightness into her voice, tried unsuccessfully to return the unexpected smile. It would have been a provisional proposal, of course, solely dependent on the result of her test. She swallowed the sudden, inane bubble of laughter that threatened to engulf her.

'Yes,' he admitted, a muscle flickering along his jaw.

'It wouldn't work. It would be for all the wrong reasons.'

'I'm very fond of you, Clemency,' he said quietly.

Her eyes searched his face. 'Yes, I think you probably are.' But he didn't love her. And there was a world of difference in the two emotions. 'But it isn't enough, is it?' How long would it take before he bitterly started to regret the sham marriage, started to resent it—and her? 'It wouldn't be fair on anyone.'

He made no attempt to dispute the fact. 'I still want

to be involved, Clemency. I want to be part of our son or daughter's life, and I don't just mean financially.'

She nodded, the lump in her throat making it impossible to speak. Once again he'd taken it for granted that her pregnancy was a fact, that their lives would be now irrevocably linked, if not shared.

She opened the front door and then paused, gazing back over her shoulder at the tall, receding figure. Ignoring the turning into his own drive, he strode past and disappeared into the night.

She felt as if she'd spent the night in a sandstorm, her eyes red and gritty from lack of sleep, her head throbbing. Her hands clasped around a mug of tea, Clemency gazed up at the kitchen clock. The surgery would be opening just about now.

One phone call and her whole life could be changed for ever. Beads of perspiration washed her body, panic twisting through her and then releasing its grip. Single parenthood was hardly ideal, but she would cope. Thousands of women did and she was more fortunate than most—would have the emotional support of both her parents, after their initial shock, and the practical support of her child's father.

One phone call. Her hands clammy, she set the mug back down on the table and pressed her fingers to her aching temples. If one day Joshua actually fell in love again, wanted to get married how would that woman react to the news that he was living next door to the single mother of his child? How could either of them stand it? The situation would be like a black comedy, completely untenable. She would sell the cottage, move back to London near her parents.

One phone call. Slowly she rose to her feet and forced her shaky legs down the hall. She felt sick, her stomach churning as if she were on a rollercoaster. Eyes dark with apprehension, she picked up the telephone and punched in the number.

'Are you sure?' she queried a few moments later, her strained voice unnaturally high-pitched. 'There couldn't be a mistake?'

No mistake, she was gently but firmly assured.

As if she were in a trance, Clemency replaced the receiver. Hadn't some part of her always known deep down exactly what the result would be? Strange, but she didn't feel anything, all her emotions deadened as if they'd been anaesthetised.

She stared unseeingly at the wall. She ought to go and finish packing, had booked a taxi for early afternoon to take her to the station.

But first she was going to have to face Joshua. It was so tempting simply to write a note, slip it through his door and slink away without actually seeing him, without actually having to witness his reaction to the news. But she owed him more than that.

Her eyes slid to the hall mirror. She looked a wreck. Huge shadows under her eyes, her skin drained of colour. Turning her back on her reflection, she picked up her key and walked out of the front door. If she didn't get this over and done with straight away, she would weaken and take the coward's course.

Joshua opened the door almost immediately she rang the bell, his drawn face indicating that he had spent an equally sleepless night.

'You've had the result,' he said without preamble, his

eyes moving over her tense face as he stood aside to allow her into the hall and closed the door.

'Yes,' she said brightly, and burst into tears.

Wordlessly he took hold of her hand and drew her into his arms.

'I'm sorry,' she mumbled as he pressed her head into the crook of his shoulder, his fingers brushing soothingly through her soft tumble of red curls. This wasn't helping at all, she thought despairingly through the salty blur. 'I'm all right now,' she insisted, lifting her head, giving him a watery smile.

There was no answering smile as he released her, his face above hers gaunt, his eyes oddly lifeless. But then, of course, he still didn't know; she still hadn't actually told him.

She took a deep breath. Oh, no, she could feel the tears welling in her eyes again.

'There isn't going to be a baby,' she blurted out.

For a second she thought he hadn't heard her, and then she flinched, the anger in his eyes momentarily incomprehensible before the truth dawned.

'No!' She denied the accusation in his eyes. How could he think even for a second that she would ever have contemplated that option? 'I mean I'm not pregnant.'

She swung away, couldn't bear to see the relief that would now be flooding his face.

'The result was negative?'

'Yes,' she mumbled.

'Clemency?' He touched her shoulder.

Slowly she turned back to face him.

Eyebrows drawn in a dark line across his forehead,

his eyes moved over her tear-stained face. 'I don't understand…'

'Why I'm not opening the champagne?' He'd expected her to be as relieved as he was. How could this
perceptive, astute man be so incredibly dense? 'I wanted
the baby.' Her eyes blazed into his. 'I wanted it.'

That she'd actually managed to disconcert Joshua
Harrington, throw him completely off-balance, gave her
no satisfaction at all.

'Oh, work it out for yourself.' She flung the words at
him, and, spinning round, wrenched open the front door
and bolted out of the house.

He made no attempt to catch up with her as she sped
down the drive. Neither had she expected him to. Not
after that little bombshell. She cringed, warmth suffo-
cating her, the surge of anger that had prompted her
indiscretion gone. She hadn't exactly told him she loved
him, but she might just as well have. No wonder he'd
looked so stunned. Oh, God, what had possessed her to
make that admission? Just about the last one Joshua
would want to hear.

Head bowed, eyes fixed on the ground, she didn't see
the figure hovering on her doorstep until she reached it.

'David, what on earth are you doing here?'

'Peace offering.' He thrust a small posy of flowers
into her hands.

'They're lovely. Thank you.' the words were automatic, like those of a well-trained parrot.

Opening the door, she tried desperately hard to concentrate on David's words as he explained that he'd
driven down to his parents the previous evening for a
family celebration.

'I'm on my way back to London now and thought I'd

just pop round on the off chance you were in.' He followed her into the hall. 'I hated the way we parted
last time.'

'I've been meaning to phone you.' The haze began to
clear in her head.

'Does that mean I'm forgiven?'

'Oh, David, of course.' The past or Simon didn't matter a jot any more. Nothing seemed to matter any more.

'You look terrible by the way,' he commented.

'Thanks.' She tried to smile but couldn't.

'Want to tell Uncle David all about it?'

She shook her head. 'Can I have a lift up to London
with you?' She would cancel the taxi, finish her packing
in record time. Just wanted to be gone from the cottage,
away from Joshua as soon as possible.

'You've decided to run away with me after all?'

'Idiot.' *No. I'm just running away full stop.*

'Though come to think of it my fiancée might raise a
few objections.'

She stared up at him. 'You've asked Jane to marry
you? And she's accepted? Oh, David, I'm so pleased.'
She gave him a swift hug. 'Congratulations.' In that moment she became aware of the shadow that had fallen
across the hall. Turning round instinctively, she saw
Joshua standing in the open doorway, the jacket she'd
left behind in the marquee last night held loosely in one
lean hand.

'Hello, David,' he greeted the other man casually as
wordlessly Clemency took hold of the jacket.

'I picked it up first thing this morning.' The blue eyes
were inscrutable as they trapped hers. 'I intended to give
it to you earlier on,' he continued easily.

But she'd fled from his house before he'd had a

chance to do so. Clemency broke his gaze, the nails of her fingers digging into her palms. He was standing there in front of her with his habitual self-assurance, in complete command of himself, giving nothing away, his voice, his expression, his whole manner suggesting that she had simply popped in earlier for an innocuous chat and a coffee. And she wanted to reach out and shake him until his teeth rattled.

Her eyes jerked back to his face. Why are you really here, Joshua Harrington? she challenged silently. Why did you remember something as trivial as my jacket, bother to walk down and fetch it for me? Just a neighbourly gesture?

'If you'll excuse me, I have to finish my packing.' She didn't quite slam the door in his face but as near as dammit.

'Don't say a word,' she cautioned David threateningly as she saw his startled expression. Face set, she started up the stairs.

'You're besotted with him, aren't you?' David mused thoughtfully.

'Not one word!' She glared down at him. 'No, I'm not besotted.' That made her sound as mindless as a lump of jelly. 'Yes.' Weakly she sat down on a stair. 'Yes, I am,' she repeated almost to herself. Totally and utterly besotted. 'I never felt like this about Simon.' She looked at David helplessly. 'I've never felt like this about anyone in my life.'

'Does he know?' David joined her on the stair.

'Mmm.' She buried her face in her hands for a moment. She could hardly have spelt it out more clearly.

'And he doesn't feel the same?' David said slowly.

'Joshua Harrington professes to being fond of me.'

She leapt to her feet. '*Fond* of me! As if I were a pet cat or dog.' She aimed a ferocious kick at the side of the staircase and yelped. 'And now I've probably broken my toe.' She turned and raced up the rest of the stairs, her throat burning with the effort of holding back another flood of tears until she reached the sanctity of her bedroom.

CHAPTER NINE

HER second weekend in Paris. Throwing back the bed clothes, Clemency padded across the thick carpet and pulled the curtains over the glass door leading out onto the small balcony. After a fortnight, the view still took her by surprise, the Eiffel Tower so close that she felt she could almost reach out a hand and touch it.

Crossing the large hotel room again, she lifted up the telephone and dialled room service, ordered breakfast and then headed for the connecting bathroom for a swift shower.

Last weekend she'd played tourist. Armed with a guide book, she'd visited all the famous landmarks, much to the amusement of her well-travelled colleagues who, having already made innumerable visits to the French capital, had become blasé about its more obvious attractions.

They had been equally amused by her determination to walk to work each morning instead of jumping in a taxi for the short trip across the river to the commercial bank situated just off the Champs-Elysées.

She had taken their gentle teasing in good part, appreciating their concerted efforts to make her feel a welcomed and valued member of the team. Nevertheless, she admitted, it would take time before she really felt part of the closely knit group, to be able to appreciate the inevitable in jokes and catch-phrases that left her feeling unintentionally excluded at times.

Rubbing her freshly washed hair with a towel, she sat down on the edge of her bed. Everything took time. She would even forget about Joshua in time. Wouldn't she? After all she could hardly expect a miracle cure in a few weeks. Abruptly she jumped to her feet and started dressing, deliberately concentrating on her plans for the day ahead.

She'd been contemplating visiting the Louvre but the lure of the sunshine outside was too tempting. She'd explore some of the parks and gardens, she decided, leave the art gallery for a wet day. And tomorrow she'd arranged to go to Versailles with a couple of her colleagues.

Slipping a sleeveless cream T-shirt over her head, she fastened the zip of her cinnamon cotton skirt, the casual clothes a welcome respite from the formal suits she donned in the week.

'*Entrez,*' she called out in response to the tap at her door.

A smartly attired maid entered the room and set the breakfast tray down on the table by the window.

'*Merci.*' Clemency exchanged smiles with the girl as she disappeared silently back into the corridor. Pulling back a chair, she sat down and took a sip of freshly squeezed orange juice, frowning as her eyes alighted on the postcard resting on the hotel stationery pad beside the tray, addressed to the twins. She still hadn't posted it yet, still hesitated from doing so, uncertain of its reception. Would Tommy be pleased or upset to receive it?

She swallowed a mouthful of croissant and stared out of the window. She was in the heart of one of the most beautiful cities in the world, staying in an all-expense-paid luxury hotel where her every need was catered for, with a job that was both absorbing and financially very well rewarded.

She closed her eyes. And right now she would trade it all in to be sitting in her back garden, breathing in the clean country air, listening to the sound of childish voices, superseded by an occasional deeper rumble, floating over the fence from next door.

Snap out of it, she ordered herself brusquely, automatically rising to her feet to pick up the clamouring telephone on her bedside table.

'Good morning, Mrs Adams,' the multi-lingual receptionist greeted her with a faultless accent. 'There is a Mr Harrington in Reception who wishes to see you.'

'Mr Harrington?' Clemency repeated incredulously, sinking onto the bed before her legs gave way. Dumbly she stared disbelievingly down at the receiver.

'Mrs Adams?'

'Right, yes.' She roused herself quickly. 'W-would you ask him to wait in the coffee lounge and I'll be down shortly? Thank you.' Joshua here in Paris? At this very moment downstairs waiting for her? Adrenalin pumped around her body, and galvanised into action she darted across to the dressing table. Swiftly she ran a comb through her still damp curls and then picked up her lipstick. She put it down again. Her hands were shaking too much.

Joshua here in Paris! There could be any number of other reasons for his presence in the capital, she warned her reflection. Just think of one, the girl with flushed cheeks and glowing eyes challenged back with an idiotic grin.

She couldn't wait for the lift. Leaving her room,

Clemency tore down the three flights of thickly carpeted stairs, forcing herself to slow down as she reached the foyer. Taking a jerky breath, she approached the coffee lounge.

She spotted him straight away. A newspaper balanced on a dark, tailored knee, he was sitting in the far corner, a tray of coffee on the low table beside him. Unobserved, she moved slowly towards him, her eyes devouring every familiar contour of his rugged face.

He lifted his head and saw her. For a second his face was completely expressionless, his eyes locking into hers across the room, and then his mouth curved into a slow, lazy smile. Tossing his newspaper aside, he rose to his full height, towering over her as she reached his side.

'Hello,' she said weakly, slipping into the chair he drew out for her. 'What are you doing here?' She couldn't take her eyes from his face, anticipation making her feel slightly dizzy as she waited for his answer.

'The twins are on half-term and I brought them over on Tuesday to see their grandparents.'

He'd been here since Tuesday? 'Their grandparents?' she said unsteadily.

'Laura's parents,' he explained easily. 'Her father's working in Paris for a couple of years.'

'Oh.' The warm bubble exploded inside her. 'I didn't know.'

'No reason why you should. They've taken the boys to Euro Disney for the day as their last big treat before we fly home tomorrow. Have you had breakfast?' he added courteously as a waiter approached them.

She nodded, eyes fixed steadfastly on the table. 'Just a *café au lait*, please.' She wished desperately that Anna had mentioned that her parents lived in Paris so that she could have been spared this appalling sense of deflation. She'd never even thought about the twins' maternal grandparents, who were doubtlessly as attached to their grandsons as Joshua's own parents.

She raised her eyes as Joshua ordered the white coffee in fluent French. His presence in Paris might be explained, but why exactly had he come to see her? Just a friendly gesture? Their parting had hardly been amicable. Because he'd been at a loose end without the twins?

'So how are you getting on?' he enquired.

'Loving every minute of it,' she said enthusiastically, and saw something flicker in his eyes, but the expression was too fleeting to analyse.

'Had much chance to explore Paris?' he drawled idly as the waiter placed a tray in front of Clemency.

'Mmm. Notre-Dame, Sacré-Coeur, Montmartre.' Her eyes dropped to the lean hands as he reached out and picked up his own cup.

'I was wondering if you'd like to drive out to Giverny this morning,' he murmured casually. 'I've hired a car.'

'Giverny?' she repeated cautiously. 'To see Monet's house?'

'Of course, if you've made other plans for the day...'

Clemency hesitated, her mind whirling in confused circles as she studied her coffee. If she had a grain of sense, she would refuse the invitation, invent a pressing engagement instead of prolonging this agony. But when had she ever been sensible about Joshua?

'Nothing special,' she heard herself murmur weakly, and took a hasty sip from her cup. Conscious of the blue eyes on her averted face, she lifted her head, must have caught him off-guard because the expression in his eyes sent a trickle of warmth scudding down her spine.

'How did you find out where I was staying?' she asked suddenly. For the first time she noticed the lines of tension etched around his straight mouth. Barely visible but very definitely there.

'I called the bank on Tuesday. You were in a meeting so I left a contact number.' He paused, the inflection in his voice changing slightly. 'Didn't you get the message?'

'No.' He'd called her on Tuesday, the day he'd arrived in Paris. 'I'm surprised anyone told you which hotel I was staying in.'

'It took a little persuasion,' he conceded with a swift grin. 'Shall we make a move?'

Her heart pounding, Clemency nodded, slipping her shoulder bag over her arm as she rose to her feet. After settling the bill, Joshua guided her from the lounge, across the foyer and through a side exit into the car park.

As he unlocked the door of the hire-car and held open the passenger door, Clemency's eyes alighted on the contents of the grocery box on the back seat. Bread, cheese, wonderful ripe salad tomatoes and a bottle of red wine. The perfect, simple ingredients for an alfresco lunch.

'Thought we might have a picnic by the river,' Joshua drawled, following her gaze.

She looked at him thoughtfully as he started up the engine. He'd been very certain that she would accept his invitation.

'Why didn't you telephone the hotel?' she asked as the car slid into the street.

He didn't answer and she assumed that he was con-

centrating on the traffic as he crossed the bridge and
eased his way into the flow of cars on the Champs-
Elysées, heading in the direction of the Arc de
Triomphe. Then as she shot him a quick glance she saw
the uncharacteristic hesitancy on his face.

'You assumed that I had received your message at the
bank,' she said quietly. And had deliberately not called
him back, hadn't wanted to see him.

He shrugged slightly.

'Why are you really here in Paris?' she suddenly demanded, infuriated by the dismissive shrug. If this
half-term trip had been planned weeks ago, the twins
would certainly have mentioned it, she thought with
growing conviction.

His eyes never strayed from the road.

'Work it out for yourself,' he said gruffly.

'Stop the car,' Clemency ordered. She was sick of
playing games with him.

'Here?' he queried mildly.

'Right here!'

Obligingly he indicated his intention and did exactly
that.

'I don't want to work it out for myself.' Oblivious to
the hooting horns behind them, she glared up at him. 'I
want you to tell me!'

'Now?' The expression in the blue eyes made her feel
dizzy.

'Right now.'

'I love you,' he said quietly.

She looked at him idiotically. 'Tell me again.'

'Can I drive on first?' he enquired hopefully.

Clemency looked out of the back window at the
stream of traffic that had ground to a halt behind them.

'Might be an idea,' she conceded, seeing the two gendarmes beginning to thread their way towards them through the stationary vehicles. She gave them both an ecstatic smile as the car slid smoothly forward, was still smiling ecstatically as Joshua turned into a side street and drew the car to a legal halt in a parking slot.

Wordlessly, he unfastened both their seat belts and, framing her face with his hands, looked down into her upturned face. 'I love you, Clemency Adams,' he said quietly. 'But you've known that for a long time, haven't you?'

'Yes,' she whispered huskily. Some part of her had always known, just as she'd always known that she loved him.

'I was just too much of a damn coward ever to admit it, not just to you but to myself. I was so damn determined never to fall in love again, so convinced that I was completely self-sufficient, that I didn't need anyone.'

'Been there. Done that. Can't risk it again,' Clemency said softly, understanding only too well.

'Something like that.' The expression in his eyes as they moved over her face made her head spin. 'If I hadn't been married that night we first met...'

'I know,' she said unsteadily.

'I went back there the next day, sat on the same bench,' he suddenly muttered.

She stared at him. 'So did I,' she confessed weakly. 'And I felt so guilty, as if I was betraying Simon, even though...' She hesitated. 'Did you love Laura very much?'

'I thought so once, but whatever I felt for her it wasn't enough to last a lifetime,' he said steadily. 'Maybe it was only ever infatuation on both sides. The twins weren't responsible for the break-up of our marriage, they were just the final catalyst.' He paused. 'But Laura will always be the boys' mother and I'll always care what happens to her.'

She nodded, wouldn't have expected anything else from him. Anna, she reflected, had mistaken that caring for something else.

'God, I've missed you so much the last couple of weeks!' he suddenly muttered, and, closing his eyes, hugged her so fiercely she gasped for breath.

'So have I,' she told him when she caught her breath again.

'Even though you've been loving every minute?' he enquired softly.

She stretched out a hand and touched his face. 'My career has always been a compensation for my failed marriage. No more. It's never been more important than you.' She smiled up into his eyes. 'But then I think I made that pretty clear to you on one other occasion, didn't I?'

'Were you really disappointed about the baby?' he asked softly.

'Terribly,' she said simply, and the expression in his eyes made her heart twist.

'So was I,' he said gruffly. 'That's what finally made me admit just how much you meant to me, how much I loved you.'

'So why didn't you tell me?' she asked shakily.

'You rushed out of the house before I'd had a chance.'

She frowned. 'Is that why you came round later?'

'You mean after I'd worked it out for myself?' he teased.

'It wasn't just to bring my jacket back, was it?'

'No,' he said quietly. 'I came to tell you what I should have realised the night you were in my bed, what I should have realised weeks ago. That I loved you. That I wanted to wake up every morning with you in my arms for the rest of my life.'

'So what stopped you?' Clemency said huskily, the image his words had conjured up making her weak.

'David was there,' he reminded her ruefully. 'I came back later after I saw his car had gone, but the house was empty and I realised that you must have left with him.'

'He gave me a lift to my parents.' If only she'd stuck to her original plan and travelled up to London by train in the afternoon! 'Why didn't you write to me care of the bank, or telephone?'

'I wrote you dozens of letters and tore them all up,' he confessed. 'And picked up the telephone hundreds of times and put it down again. I needed to see you face to face.' He paused. 'If it hadn't been for the twins I'd have caught the first flight to Paris the day after you left. But I couldn't just leave them, not so soon after Jamie had come out of hospital.'

'So you waited until half-term, when Jamie was fit enough to travel and he and Tommy could come with you?'

He nodded. 'I was so terrified I'd left it too late,' he muttered.

'Oh, Josh,' she said softly, her hands curling around his neck as she reached for his mouth.

'Um, I think we might have an audience,' Joshua murmured some time later.

She opened her eyes, and smiled blissfully at the

group of giggling girls walking by on the pavement. Paris was a city for lovers after all.

'And neither have I any intention of proposing to you in a back street,' Joshua announced firmly, reaching for his seat belt.

Clemency stood on the Japanese bridge at Giverny, gazing over the water lily pond, immortalised for ever in Monet's paintings. Hand in hand she and Joshua had sauntered around the gardens of the rosy-bricked, green-shuttered house where the impressionist had spent much of his life, his home now preserved as a museum.

'Happy?' Joshua murmured by her side.

She turned to look up at him. 'I'd be happy wherever I was, as long as I was with you,' she said simply.

'You will marry me?' he demanded gruffly.

'Yes, please.' The silent pledge in his eyes as they locked into hers made her reach out for the railing. All his tomorrows for the rest of his life.

'More flowers for you, Mrs Harrington.'

Propped up in the hospital bed, Clemency smiled as the plump, cheerful auxiliary bustled into the room, carrying two bouquets which she held out for Clemency's inspection.

'How lovely.' Drinking in the scent of the exquisite blooms, Clemency examined the accompanying cards. One from the newly-weds, David and Jane. The other from Anna and her fiancé, now a junior partner in the local veterinary practice.

'I'll go and put them in water.' The auxiliary started for the door, exchanging greetings with the broad-shouldered man who'd just entered the room, ushering in two hesitant small boys ahead of him.

'Hello.' Tommy and Jamie surveyed Clemency with large, solemn eyes from the foot of the bed.

'Come here.' She held open her arms, and with face-splitting grins they rushed to hug her. Over their dark heads her eyes met the dark blue ones, their expression making words superfluous.

'I've brought you a present.' Tommy carefully placed a jam jar on the bedside table and unfastened the lid.

Clemency surveyed the wriggling black specks. 'Tadpoles,' she said enthusiastically. What else could she have expected? 'They're wonderful, Tommy. Thank you.'

'You can't keep them for ever,' he told her earnestly. ''Cause they'll have to go back to the pond when they're bigger.' He glanced resignedly at his father.

Clemency nodded obediently and turned her attention to the parcel Jamie was thrusting into her hand.

'I made it 'specially for you. Thought it might be useful,' he said nonchalantly.

Carefully Clemency undid the wrapping and inspected the two yoghurt cartons, daubed with blue and orange paint, stuck together with tape. 'I think this is going to be extremely useful,' she agreed gravely.

Jamie beamed with pride.

'Thank you very much.' She hugged him again. She loved him as dearly as she did Tommy, treasured each twin's uniqueness.

'Here she is.' The door opened and a nurse wheeled in a cot, placing it carefully by the bed.

Slowly the twins approached and gazed down at the tiny infant.

Tommy didn't say a word, a look of utter entrancement crossing his face.

'She's quite nice,' Jamie observed, and, dropping to his small haunches, began to examine the base of the cot with a professional eye.

'She's bought you both a little present.' Retrieving from her locker the two packages which she'd purchased several weeks ago, Clemency handed them to the twins.

'She's been shopping? On her own?' Jamie looked visibly impressed, his half-sister evidently going up a notch in his estimation.

'Thank you very much. It's very kind of you,' Tommy said politely, peering into the cot. 'Next time I come in I'm going to bring you a present,' he promised. He lowered his voice confidentially. 'Something very, very special.'

'Frisk him before he sets a foot inside the hospital tomorrow,' Clemency muttered imploringly to Joshua.

'Will do,' he returned with a grin.

Squatting down on the carpet, the twins began to investigate their parcels. A beautifully illustrated wildlife book for the embryo naturalist, and a model construction kit for the budding engineer.

Taking advantage of their distraction, Joshua sat down on the side of the bed and greeted Clemency properly for the first time with a long, lingering kiss. Then simultaneously their eyes dropped to the sleeping baby. How could you possibly love someone so much when you've only known them for a day? Clemency thought with a renewed surge of wonder.

'Oh, Lord, another redhead,' Joshua groaned in her ear.

'You're going to have to come up with a different

line,' his wife reproved him. 'You used that one yester-day.' Never as long as she lived would she forget the expression on Joshua's face as he'd held their daughter in his arms for the first time. An expression that now seemed to have been replaced by one of infinite smug-ness.

'Laura phoned last night,' he said softly. 'Sends her love and congratulations.'

Clemency smiled. She'd met Laura for the first time shortly before their marriage. She'd been dreading it—an ex-wife and future wife had seemed like a recipe for disaster—but after some initial awkwardness she had discovered to her relief and surprise that she genuinely liked the other woman who had reminded her in so many ways of Anna, and who'd showed absolutely no resent-ment at Clemency's involvement in her sons' lives.

'I was just never cut out for motherhood,' she'd said candidly, and had paused, her voice breaking slightly. 'Just look after them, love them in the way I never could. And don't let them forget me completely.'

Clemency's heart squeezed with compassion, remem-bering the wistfulness in Laura's eyes.

'Are you getting tired, darling?' Joshua looked down at her with concern.

She shook her head. 'Just thinking how lucky I am.' Eyes swimming with love, she gazed up at him. 'We really ought to decide on a name.'

'Ruth.' Tommy scrambled onto the bed and put an arm around her neck.

'Mary.' Jamie scrambled up on the other side and slid his fingers through hers.

'Eleanor.' Joshua's hand tightened across her shoulder.

'Serendipity Sapphire,' Clemency murmured dreamily.

The three most important males in her life looked at her aghast.

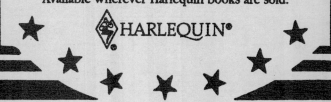

Presents
Extravaganza
25 YEARS!

It's our birthday and we're celebrating....

Twenty-five years of romance fiction
featuring men of the world and captivating women—
Seduction and passion guaranteed!

Not only are we promising you three months of terrific
books, authors and romance, but as an added **bonus**
with the retail purchase of two Presents® titles,
you can receive a special one-of-a-kind keepsake.
It's our gift to you!

Look in the back pages of any Harlequin Presents® title,
from May to July 1998, for more details.

Available wherever Harlequin books are sold.

◆ HARLEQUIN®

Take 2 bestselling love stories FREE

Plus get a FREE surprise gift!

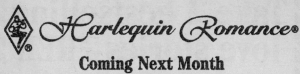

Coming Next Month

#3515 THE DIAMOND DAD Lucy Gordon
Garth had promised his wife diamonds for their tenth anniversary—
Faye didn't want diamonds, she wanted a divorce! But with two gorgeous
children and his beautiful wife at stake, Garth was determined to do all
he could to save his family!

The Big Event! *One special occasion—that changes your life forever.*

#3516 HEAVENLY HUSBAND Carolyn Greene
It seemed incredible, but when Kim's ex-fiancé Jerry woke from his
accident he seemed like a totally different man. Instead of a womanizing
workaholic, he'd become the perfect hero. He said she was in danger,
and that she needed his protection. But the only danger Kim could
foresee was that maybe heaven *was* missing an angel—and they'd want
him back!

Guardian Angels: *Falling in love sometimes needs a little help from
above!*

#3517 THE TROUBLE WITH TRENT! Jessica Steele
When Trent de Havilland waltzed into Alethea's life, she was already
wanting to leave home. So Trent's idea that she move in with him could
have been the ideal solution. But Alethea's trouble with Trent wasn't so
much that she was living with him, but that she was falling in love with
him!

Look out also for another great **Whirlwind Weddings** title:

#3518 THE MILLION-DOLLAR MARRIAGE Eva Rutland
Tony Costello only found out about his bride's fortune after their
whirlwind romance had ended in a trip to the altar. He couldn't forgive
her for being rich and for keeping it a secret. Melody had deliberately
tried to conceal her true worth for the sake of Tony's pride; now she
would have to fight to save their marriage. Rich or poor, she loved
Tony—she was just going to have to prove it!

Whirlwind Weddings: *who says you can't hurry love?*